MURDER MONDAY

Kathleen S. Allen

ISBN: 9781076786128

Imprint: Independently published

Chapter One

The jangling ringtone of some obscure rock band song woke me from a sound sleep. I froze, watching the phone jiggle across my bedside table. Either someone was hurt or dead. It was never a good idea to answer a phone call in the middle of the night. I fumbled for the phone placed next to the bed on the bedside table but in my haste to get to it I managed to dump my water bottle and water spilled onto the paperback book I had been reading. And me. "SHIT!" I yelled grabbing the phone before it got too drenched. I wiped it on my nightshirt before answering.

"Hello?" I dabbed at the water with my pillow, now fully awake. After cleaning most of the spill, I walked barefoot to the bathroom to turn on the light and to get a towel.

"Mel? Jessie is missing. I've called her cell so many times her voice mail is full. No one has seen her in days. She was supposed to come home from college tonight. I expected her at seven. It's now after midnight and she's not here. Can you help?"

"Have you called the police?" I asked attempting to sop up the rest of the water.

There was a huge wet spot on my nightshirt. Now I'd have to change. I threw the wet pillow toward the laundry basket. It landed on top of the pile, making it wobble precariously. I shifted so that the phone was in the other hand. I got the wet nightshirt partially off, switched hands again and stood shivering in the night breeze coming through the window.

"Yes, I called the police," Cindy said. She enunciated each word slowly as if I would not be capable of understanding speech. "One of the cops told me she probably went away for a long weekend with her boyfriend. She doesn't even have a boyfriend." Cindy sobbed the last words out. Moving with what I call panther stealth I tiptoed-limped to the closet and opened the door to get a robe out. Quietly shutting the door I slipped the robe on, switched the phone to my other hand and sat back on the bed. The end of the bed wasn't wet. I listened but there was only silence.

"Hello? Cindy? You there?"

"Yes, where else would I be? What were you doing just now?"

"I had to put a robe on, my nightshirt was wet. Try not to worry. We'll find her."

"I'm not going to go there, are you alone? Oh my God, I forgot to ask if Byron was there. I'm just so…" She stopped talking.

"No, Byron isn't here. I told you we broke up right after I left the force. Look, let me make a couple of calls and get back to you. Call me immediately if Jessie comes home or contacts you in any way, okay?"

"Okay, thanks, Mel. I need to call John, Joan, and Joey to let them know she's missing. I should've called them first, I guess. It's just that you being a cop and all…" she let her voice trail off.

"Former cop," I said. "You haven't called them yet?" Partial relief washed over me. "She's probably with one of them; call me right back after you talk to each one." I crossed my fingers for luck. Not that I had much. Luck that is.

"You're right, I bet she went out to San Francisco to visit Joey, you know how much they get along.. I'll call you back." She hung up and so did I. Jessie is a smart girl; she wouldn't just take off without telling someone. I hoped that someone was one of her siblings. But, I had a gut feeling. Not one I liked. Hunches. I got them as a cop and I was always right. This time I hoped I wasn't.

I padded downstairs sans cane, I used the stairway railing instead. Yawning, I looked at the clock. After one in the morning. Too late to make any calls tonight. I got a drink of water, took a pain pill and headed back upstairs. I paused on the stairs taking deep breaths until the spasms in my leg subsided. I climbed the stairs slowly hoping the pain pill would work a miracle and actually allow me to sleep pain-free. I doubted I'd get much sleep anyway. I hoped Cindy found Jessie safe and sound, I really did. Poor Cindy, first her husband dies, then Jessie was in trouble and now this. *Her luck is worse than mine.*

I changed my sheets and lay down on my left side pulling my knees up to my chest. It was the only position I could lay in that allowed me any relief. I lay thinking about Jessie, waiting for the pain to dissipate and sleep to come. I wanted Jessie to be okay. I wanted to be back a year ago before the shooting. I wanted Byron back in my bed and in my life. I closed my eyes drifting off. The pain med doing its thing.

The next thing I knew it was morning and for one shining moment I felt at peace. Then all hell broke loose.

Pounding on my front door. “Mel?” I got up too quickly; a wave of dizziness assaulted me as I held onto the nightstand waiting for the dizziness to pass. The pounding continued.

“Mel? Let me in, Mel!” *Cindy.* I had fallen asleep with the robe on. I pulled it tighter as I made my way down the stairs gripping the railing trying not to favor my leg. I took the chain off, unlocked the door and opened it.

Cindy stood there crying. She shoved something at me as she pushed past me coming inside. I noticed the neighbors getting ready to start their day. Rob, dressed in his banking suit waved at me from across the way as his garage doors opened; Maureen in her green scrubs nodded as she got into her car. I waved back. Sighing, I shut the door limping to where Cindy stood. I unfolded the newspaper she handed me.

Student Jumps to Death-read the headline.

Oh, no! It can't be Jessie!

My heart sank as I skimmed the article. I made my way to the sofa and gestured to Cindy she should sit too. She perched on the edge of a chair still crying but softly as a wounded animal might cry. I looked up at her at one point but she pointed to the article in my hand.

"No, read it. All of it, then we can talk." I longed for a cup of coffee. No, two. Two cups of coffee and a bagel is my usual breakfast fare. One of my medications made me so sleepy I needed extra caffeine just to function like a regular person. Trying to focus, I read the article.

College student, Jessie Lewis was found at the bottom of the Tower Building earlier today. Sources close to her say she was despondent after learning her grades were not as high as she wanted. These same sources say she was having "boyfriend troubles" but would not elaborate further. The family states that funeral arrangements are pending.

I looked up at Cindy.

"She didn't jump," Cindy said and took a deep breath. "She'd never jump. She'd never go up to the roof a building. She hated to stand on a step ladder. Someone forced her up there. Someone pushed her off."

"This is terrible, I'm so sorry."

"The police came to my door right after I called you to tell me the news. I had to go down to the morgue to identify her body. It was Jessie. She looked so sweet, like she was sleeping. I held her hand until the officers pulled me away. I'm never going to see my baby again, am I?" She started crying again. I limped over to the downstairs bathroom and grabbed a box of tissues. I handed them to her.

"Did you call the kids?" She shook her head.

"I didn't have the heart to tell them. Can you call them?"

I nodded. "I'll call John, he can tell Joey and Joan." Instead of an answer she buried her face in the tissue as fresh sobs shook her body.

I had all of them on speed dial. I opened my phone and called John, the eldest first."This is John," he said. I called his work number because I knew he usually went in early. As a loan officer at a bank he wanted to make a good impression.

"Hey, John, it's Mel," I said, trying not to keep my voice too light. I hated to do this over the phone but I wasn't in any shape to drive all the way downtown, find a parking space and then walk blocks to Beechton Bank. Just the thought of it made my leg ache in sympathy.

"Mel, what's up? I haven't heard from you in a while. How you doing? Mom said you are still in a lot of pain."

"True. Look, John, are you sitting down?"

"Yes, why? What's going on? Your voice sounds funny." I sighed. Damn it! I took a deep breath to steady myself.

"Have you seen the newspaper this morning?"

"No, why?"

"John, I'm sorry but there's no easy way to say this. Jessie is dead."

"Dead? What do you mean, dead? She can't be dead. I just talked to her." Why do family members always say that? My head hurt and felt like it was going to burst at the seams. Telling family members their relative was dead was never my favorite part of being a cop. It was doubly hard when it was a friend. I massaged my temple with one hand.

"You're wrong," he said with emphasis as if saying the words strong enough would make it less true.

"She was found this morning at the bottom of the Tower Building on campus. The police think she jumped."

"How did you find out it's her?" I glanced at Cindy who still sobbed into her tissue.

"It's her, John. Your mom went to the morgue this morning."

"Oh my…where's mom now? Is she with you?"

"Yes, she's sitting right here with me, want to talk to her?" I looked over at Cindy who finished crying. She held out her hand for the phone. I got up gingerly. I handed the phone to her on my way to the kitchen in order to give her some privacy. I leaned against the counter for a moment. I needed to be strong for Cindy and her kids. I couldn't break down, not now. *Keep it together, Thompson.* I used the single-cup coffeemaker to brew myself a cup. I took my usual handful of morning pills and waited for the coffee to brew. Once it finished I gulped the pills down with a swallow of coffee. Cindy came into the kitchen looking sad but no longer crying.

"John is going to call Joan and Joey," she said. I gestured with my cup.

"Want me to brew you one?"

“Sure, do you have decaf?”

“No, sorry. But I do have some herbal tea somewhere.” I rummaged in the cupboard until I found the tea.

She eyed the box. “How old is that, Mel?”

“Tea doesn’t get old,” I said. I put the kettle on, got out a cup and limped over to the table. I sat down with my coffee taking another sip. Cindy sat across from me. Neither one of us said a word. I heard the kettle whistling. I started to get up but Cindy got up first.

“I’ll get it, I know where everything is.” I sipped my coffee watching the birds outside my window. I put a birdfeeder up just to amuse the neighborhood cats. I shifted in my chair wincing. Cindy came back in with her cup. She sat back down. “I couldn’t find the milk,” she said.

“I don’t usually buy milk, sorry.”

“You live like you’re still in college,” she scolded. “There isn’t anything edible in your ‘fridge.”

I shrugged.

“Lots of pain this morning?” she asked taking a sip of her tea.

“As usual,” I said. “I’ll be better as soon as the meds kick in.” I paused “Can I get you some food?” I asked. “There’s a takeout menu near the ‘fridge. One of the bakeries delivers. The one circled in red.”

She shook her head, “No, thanks.” She put her head in her hands and began crying again.

“It would be easier to go out,” I said. “Let’s get a bagel downtown. My treat.” She might not feel like crying so much in a public place.

She shook her head again. “I can’t, Mel. Look, I better go. I have to call everyone.”

“You don’t have to do it right now, Cindy. Stay a few minutes, please? Have another cup of coffee with me?” She went out the door without saying goodbye.

Cindy had left my phone on the table. I reached for it dialing the number of the city police by heart.

“Beechton Police, this is Barbara speaking.”

“Hi, Barbara, this is Mel Thompson.”

"Mel! How you doing? Long time no see, what's up?"

"Same old, trying to recover. Is Byron in by any chance?"

"Sure is, you know him, first one here and last one to leave." She laughed. "Let me put you through. Hang on. Good to hear your voice, Mel. Stop by sometime and I'll tell you all the juicy gossip."

"Will do, thanks." I heard a click.

"Williams." His voice smooth and professional. I grinned.

"Hi, Williams."

"Mel? How you doing? I've been meaning to call." *Yeah.*

"I'm okay. Look, I'm calling because a friend of mine lost a daughter and she doesn't think its suicide."

"I thought you were calling to hear my gorgeous voice," he joked.

"That too," I said.

"You talking about the college kid that jumped this morning?"

"Yeah, her mom is a friend of mine. You've met her, Cindy Lewis? Blonde, good looking, stacked as you put it."

"Right, the one with all the J named kids."

"Yep. She wants to know what happened."

"You know I can't reveal what we are doing to a civilian, Mel."

"Do you mean Cindy or me?"

He hesitated. "Both. You aren't a cop any more, Mel." His voice softened.

"I am aware of that," I said. I waited. He sighed audibly.

"As far as the M.E. knows she jumped. She's ruling it a suicide."

"Her mom thinks she was pushed," I said. "Said she was happy."

"Well, that would be easier to take than thinking your kid jumped off a roof intentionally, wouldn't it?"

"Can you just keep an open mind on this?" I asked, irritation creeping into my voice. Damn pain pills hadn't taken the edge off yet.

"Sure, I will. Hey, some of the guys are getting together on Friday for beer and chips at O'Malley's. Seven o'clock. See you there?"

"I'll try," I said.

"I gotta go, Mel. See you Friday." He hung up. I thought about the days when we'd both be done with the job and come home, jump into a hot shower and into the nearest bed. His or mine. It didn't matter. We were close to moving in together but something held me back. After I got shot I backed off. I heard he was dating another cop now. It hurt that he was able to move on so soon.

Get a grip, Thompson.

I put the phone down on the table. There were days when I was almost pain-free, today was not one of those days. I drank more coffee and opened my laptop to check my email. Cindy wasn't the only one who needed a distraction. I propped my leg up on a chair. Sometimes that helped. Nope. I shifted in my chair. I had lots of spam but nothing worth noting. No jobs for a gimpy former cop turned P.I. with hunches.

The front door opened and Cindy came in with two bags of groceries. I started to stand up but she breezed past me to the kitchen before I could. I sat back down.

"Did you buy out the store?" I asked.

"I just got you some essentials, milk, bread, eggs, butter. I figure you can scramble yourself some eggs for a quick meal. You're too thin, Mel."

"Yeah, pain does that to you, you don't feel like eating."

"I bought you bagels and cream cheese. There's extra too." Great. Now I had food. Guess that means I'll have to eat. Cindy brought me a bagel smeared with cream cheese. I gestured to it.

"You're not having any?"

"No, eat up, Mel." I took a bite. It was good. Suddenly hungry, I decided I would eat it after all. Maybe I was having a reverse reaction to hearing about Jessie. Cindy lost her appetite and I found mine. Odd.

"What am I going to do without Jessie?" Cindy asked as I bit into my bagel. "I was so looking forward to her coming home for a couple of days."

"Why was she coming home?" I asked. "I mean, what's wrong with her apartment?"

"I dunno. Something about having to fumigate or something." I munched my bagel trying to figure out the best way to approach what I had to say. I put the bagel down and wiped my fingers on a paper napkin.

"Look, Cindy, there's something I have to tell you about Jessie. Something I learned about her when I was a cop. Something I didn't have the heart to tell you and still don't."

Her eyes widened. "What? You're scaring me, Mel. What is it?"

"She was busted for solicitation and drugs."

"She was not!" Cindy stood up nearly knocking my bagel off its plate. She glared at me. "How dare you say something like that to me!"

"She worked as a stripper at Barre," I said. "The mayor gets it into her head that if she rounds up all the strip bar ladies, prostitution will be non-existent in our city. We raided Barre last year and there was Jessie."

Cindy sat back down, her anger gone. "What did she say?"

"She said she was earning money for college. She said she made a couple of porn films. She denied working as a prostitute, so did most of the other girls. I told her if she quit the club I wouldn't arrest her and she laughed. Said she made more money in one night there than she made in a year working on campus."

"Jessie?" Cindy seemed like a balloon that has lost its air.

"I'm sorry, Cindy. She asked me not to tell you. I said I wouldn't if she quit. She promised me she would once she made enough money to pay for the rest of her college degree," I said.

"And the drugs?"

"I caught her doing a line of Coke. I gave her a warning and she promised she'd quit that too. And as far as I know, she did. She called me right after the shooting, came to see me in the hospital. Said she quit Barre, was not doing drugs or porn any more. I believed her."

"Wait, isn't Barre the place where you got shot?" Cindy asked her hand going to her mouth.

"Yes, the very same."

"Is there, I mean was there a connection?" Cindy asked.

"If there was I never found one."

Cindy started crying again.

"I didn't know my own daughter," she sobbed. "Why didn't she come to me?"

"Because you're her mother and she loves you. She didn't want to hurt you."

"Do you think she jumped off that building?" Cindy asked in a quiet voice.

"I don't know. I haven't talked to her in weeks. I do know she was clean, had been for months. She got out of that business. I made sure of it." I didn't give Cindy the details but she guessed them anyway.

"You never told me how you got shot," she said looking at me. "Tell me what happened that night at Barre. Was Jessie there? I want the exact details. Everything." I sighed. Might as well get it over with.

Chapter Two

"Right after I confronted Jessie, I went to see the owner of Barre. I told him I was Jessie's aunt, flashed my badge and told him she quit." I sighed drinking the last of my coffee down. Someone should make a never ending cup of coffee. I wished mine would fill back up again. Cindy noticed my forlorn look at the bottom of my cup.

"Want me to make you another one?" she asked.

"Yes, please. Know how?"

"I gave one of those to Jessie her freshman year. She showed me how to use it." She was silent as she brewed me another cup. It only took a few minutes. She came back into the kitchen and handed me the freshly-brewed goodness. I started to take the cup but she pulled it back. "Your hand is shaking," she said. "Maybe you've had enough coffee." I could tell she was reluctant to give it to me. She held it just out of my reach.

"Let me have the coffee, Cindy. I need it to wake myself up. The meds make my hands shake, it has nothing to do with how much or how little caffeine I've been drinking." I stared her down using my "cop stare." Finally, she handed me the cup.

"You should wean yourself off of caffeine, it's not good for you," she said as she sat back down. "Tell me more about the shooting."

"After I talked to the owner of Barre, I thought Jessie was fine. A couple of weeks later, Jessie called to tell me she quit Barre and the porn movies. I was thrilled she actually listened to my advice. Anyway, Byron and I were on a B&E call, someone was breaking into Barre. They're closed on Mondays and this was a Monday. Byron went around the front and I went around back. I saw a smashed in window. I called for back-up and told Byron to come in the back. Almost as soon as I said those words a guy came out of nowhere shooting. He shot me in the back as I turned." I indicated my lower spine. "I fell to the ground and by then Byron was there.

He called for an ambulance. The bullet lodged near my spinal cord. One of the discs in my back is bulging and the bullet is lying next to that both of them pressing on the bundle of nerves at the base of my spine that run down my left leg. Hence the pain in my leg."

"Do you think that you telling Jessie to quit caused them to get back at you?" Cindy asked.

"Possibly. No way to know for sure. The guy that shot me took off. We couldn't find him, or rather the cops couldn't find him."

"And that's why you quit being a cop?"

"No, I quit because the docs wouldn't do surgery to take the bullet out. They said it was too close to my spinal cord and I could end up paralyzed if they tried. They figured in a few months the bullet would settle in, the nerves would be less inflamed and I'd have less pain. Meanwhile, I couldn't be a cop anymore. Or ever. I went on disability." I gestured to my bag slung over the chair in the living room. "Can you hand me my bag? I want to show you something."

"Sure, here you go," Cindy got up, grabbed the bag and handed it to me. I rummaged in it taking my wallet out.

"I just got this a couple of months ago." I held open the wallet to show her.

"Nice. What is it exactly?"

"It's my P.I. license. I applied to be a private investigator I just got the license the other day." I rubbed my hand over it. Now if only I could be able to use it.

Cindy clapped her hands together making me jump.

"What's wrong?" I asked.

"Nothing. How'd you like a job?" she asked.

"Yes, I would but I need to wait until my leg is pain-free."

"You need money, right?"

"Right," I said. I knew where this was going. I shook my head at her. "I'm not taking your money, Cindy."

"But, this is perfect. You could investigate Jessie's death as a professional, you'd have an in with the cops, they know you already." Boy, did she have the wrong idea about P.I.'s and their working relationships with cops.

"I don't want your money, Cindy." She dug in her purse and pulled out her checkbook. She took out a pen clicking it open.

"What is your retainer fee?" she asked, pen poised to write.

"I refuse to take money from you," I said. "You're my friend, my best friend. I can't take your money, Cindy. Please don't ask me too." *I'm not that desperate.*

"If you don't tell me then I'll just write a check for five thousand that should cover a few days, right?"

"Write it for five hundred and I won't cash it until I find out something." She bent over the check to write. She handed it to me. I folded it in half and stuck it in my wallet.

"You aren't even going to look at it?"

"No, and I warn you, I may find out that Jessie killed herself. Are you okay with that?"

She nodded. "I need to know what happened to her, Mel. One way or the other." She stared out the window for a moment. She looked at her watch. “I should go. Thanks for helping me, Mel. I appreciate it.” She took my plate and our cups into the kitchen. I could hear her rinsing them off before putting them in the dishwasher. She came out wiping her hands on a towel. “I bought you a turkey on rye with mayo, it’s in the ‘fridge.” She came over and kissed me on the cheek. “I’m going to miss her so much,” she said in a soft voice giving me a brief hug. “Why did this happen, Mel? Why?”

“I wish I knew, Cindy. She didn’t deserve this. And I know it doesn’t mean much right now but I promise I’ll find out who did this and make them pay.” *Jeez, I said this all the time when I was a homicide cop I didn’t realize how lame it sounded until now.*

Cindy gathered up her purse. She flung the strap over her shoulder. “I’ll call you when the kids get in. I’m sure they’ll want to see you.” Her voice caught. “I’ll let you know about the funeral arrangements too.”

"St. Matthew's?" I asked. It was the church she was married in. Her husband of twenty years had the nerve to drop dead of a heart attack two years ago. Jessie was the last bird out of the nest.

"Yes, probably. I'll ask John to call Father Mark." She walked with heavy steps to the door.

"You gonna be okay, Cindy?" I asked.

"Yes, what other choice do I have?" she replied. She paused. "Does anyone ever know anyone else? I mean, inside." The tears came again. "I thought I knew my own daughter, Mel. Oh sure, she had her problems in high school but she settled down once she started college. At least I thought she did." She laughed but her laugh was hollow. We hugged again. She held onto me as if I was her life preserver. Maybe I was.

Chapter Three

I brewed myself another cup of coffee. No new messages were on my phone. Nothing. I took the cup to the living room and sat on the chair near the window. The pain wasn't too bad if I elevated my leg so I put my left foot on the footstool. I felt the tears slide down my cheeks. *Jessie, what happened?* Wiping them away with my hand I sighed. I hadn't seen Jessie since the shooting. When she came to visit me in the hospital she looked healthy and full of life. I remember her chattering on about a new boyfriend but I was in and out of a drug-induced pain cloud so I don't recall her ever saying his name. Oh, Jess. What happened to you? Why did you jump off that building? Or did somebody push you?

The ringing of my phone jarred me out of my wallowing. Unfortunately I left my phone on the table. It took me a minute to get to it. By then the stupid thing had stopped ringing. I started at the number. Cindy. Or one of her kids. I didn't have the heart to talk to any of them right now. I sat down at the table opening my laptop. Was there a chance Jessie had died because of my interference with Barre's owner? Was I shot to keep me from investigating something going on at Barre? I decided to start a list of people I wanted to talk to. First on my list was the creep that owned Barre.

I decided a road trip was in order. I could drive if I wasn't on too many pain pills. Okay, if I wasn't on any. I didn't feel dizzy or sleepy so I thought I'd be okay. Just for good measure I downed another pain pill with my coffee. I shrugged on a jacket; the October chill was in the air.

I grabbed my keys and my cane. Hobbling out to the garage I hit the garage door opener. My bright lime green VW beetle bug hadn't seen the light of day for a few weeks. I ran my hand along the drivers-side fender. I bought it from a guy who got it from this other guy who bought it in Italy and had it shipped to the US. Only once he got it here, his wife vetoed it so he had to sell it. The guy bought it and I bought it from him. The story was probably bogus but I walked up to it when it was parked on the street and fell in love. If you can fall in love with a car, then this was true love for me.

How can anyone resist a lime green VW bug from the 1970s? I'm pretty sure it had been painted over a couple of zillion times and I planned on restoring it to its original color…someday. You know that old saying, when pigs fly? Yeah, that one. I paid cash for it after hitting the ATM and Byron up for money. The heater barely worked, the windshield washer worked when it wanted to; it held 11.1 gallons of gas, so given the price of gas these days was a heck of a lot cheaper than owning a gas-guzzling SUV. I ran the plates just to make sure it wasn't stolen and it came back clean. I added a cloth-covered, leopard-spotted steering wheel cover; the old plastic one was cold on my hands in the winter. The gray interior was fairly clean so I also added floorboard mats to keep it nice.

"Hello, Baby." I named her Baby after the Katharine Hepburn/Cary Grant movie, *Bringing up Baby* where she finds a leopard and names it Baby. Once I was in the car I panted with exertion. I hadn't been exercising much in the last year. Or rather, not at all. I laid my forehead on the steering wheel for a minute. I stayed that way so long the motion detector that stayed on long enough for you to get into your car turned off. I sighed, starting the car and put it into reverse. I steeled myself as I backed out of the garage. Sitting wasn't too painful. It was standing and walking that did me in.

The drive across town into what the townies called "the bad part of town" was shorter than I hoped. I drove past The Barre looking for a parking place in front. The closest parking spot was a good two blocks away. No freaking chance of me walking that far. I put on my turn signal and went around the block three more times. Finally, a spot in front opened up. I pulled in quickly before anyone else could. Gritting my teeth against the inevitable pain to follow I got out of the car locking it. In this neighborhood it wasn't a guarantee it would still be there when I was done but at least I felt better about it. I saw a young kid looking at the car.

"I'll give you ten bucks if you promise to watch the car for me, five now and five when I come out," I said preparing to get out my wallet. He shook his head.

"Naw, Lady. No one wanna steal that eyesore anyway." He went up some steps and disappeared into a doorway.

Miffed, I yelled at his retreating back. "Hey, this eyesore is a classic! Lots of people might want to steal it!" Realizing how stupid that sounded, I leaned against the door getting my bearings. I took a couple of deep breaths before I hauled myself up the curb. Limping up to the door I saw a big CLOSED sign hanging there. I banged on it anyway. I listened for movement inside. I thought I heard voices but no one answered the door. I banged on it with my cane and shouted.

"Open up, Barre, it's Mel Thompson." The door flew open so hard I nearly fell inside. Strong, rough hands steadied me. I looked up and up. Towering over me was one of Barre's bouncers.

"Boss wants to know what do you want?'" he asked. He was a hulking bodybuilder type with arms the size of small tree trunks and a huge neck. He wore a black tee shirt stretched across his broad chest and black skin-tight jeans tucked into black motorcycle boots with a huge silver buckle on the side. I had no doubt that the ends of the boots were reinforced with steel. His name slipped my memory.

"Thanks…uh…"

"Alejandro Lopez," he grinned at me showing me capped teeth, one with a gold insert. His bald head shone with something oily and a single diamond stud in his left ear sparkled in the early morning sunlight. Dark eyes stared at me.

"Thanks, Alejandro. Tell Mr. Barre I want to talk to him about Jessie Lewis." He winked at me before shutting the door in my face. I waited leaning on my cane for support. I wished there was a Starbucks nearby. I needed a caffeine jolt. The door opened wider and Alejandro stepped aside gesturing me to enter.

The club smelled like a combination of stale tobacco, stale beer and disinfectant. I saw several workers wiping down tables. At night the club sparkled with twinkling lights overhead, a spot on the stage and a shiny pole right in the middle of the stage. In the glare of daylight, the place looked cheap and shabby. I saw several girls huddled in a corner sunglasses on as if the feeble sunlight coming in through the half-closed drapes was too much for them. One in particular seemed interested in me. I felt her eyes on me as Alejandro led me through the main floor to a set of offices in the back. He knocked politely on one door.

"Come in," said a voice. Alejandro opened the door for me then closed it as soon as I was inside. Mr. Barre sat at a small metal desk clicking on a laptop. He closed the lid getting up to extend a hand to me. I ignored it and made my way to a rickety looking chair sitting in front of his desk. I sat down grateful to finally be sitting. He sat too."What can I do for you Officer Thompson?"

"It's Ms. Thompson, I am no longer on the force." I stared at him. "But, somehow I think you knew that. And anyway, it used to be Detective Thompson." I mean, if he's going to call me by the wrong name, it should be the right wrong name.

He toyed with a pen on his desk. "I believe I did hear something like that. Weren't you shot on the job?" He eyed my cane. "Too bad." He was a small man, with beady blue eyes sunk into his head. A comb over solidified a nod to vanity. He wore rings on every finger except his thumbs. His nose was too large for his face and the thin lips below signified a mean streak. He had trouble making decisions without his thugs around. He smiled but it was more of a grimace.

"Well, since the shooting happened in the back of your club in the alley that you own…" I let my voice trail off as I looked at him expectantly.

"And, you came here because you want to sue me? Have your lawyer call my lawyers," he stood up dismissing me. I stayed put. He sat back down. "What you do you want, Thompson? I have work to do."

"I want to know what you know about Jessie Lewis throwing herself off the Tower Building this morning."

His eyes widened in mock surprise. "Jessie killed herself? Sad," he shook his head. "If she stayed with me she'd still be alive." His eyes bored into me. I got the feeling he already knew that Jessie was dead.

"Let me get this straight, you believe that if Jessie stayed stripping for you, doing drugs and lap dances for customers she'd be better off?"

"At least she wouldn't be dead." He had a point. I nodded. He sighed. "I don't know any more than you know. I heard it from one of the girls."

My ears perked up. "Which one?"

He waved a hand in the air. "No one of consequence. She read it in the paper." He pressed a button and the door opened. Alejandro and another bodybuilder stood there. A blond one.

"If that's all you want to see me about then Alejandro and Sven will see you out, Ms. Thompson. Don't bother me again." He snapped his fingers. I waited a beat then got up. Alejandro handed me my cane. I took it but before I could put it on the floor Sven kicked it out from under me and I went down. Fuming, I hauled myself up to a sitting position with the chair. The cane lay at my feet. I reached over and used it to push myself up the rest of the way. Pain surged through my leg. I ignored it as I walked with as much dignity as I could to the door. I turned back to Barre.

"If I find out you or anyone of your minions had anything to do with Jessie's death, badge or no badge, I will make you pay," I said through clenched teeth. I brushed past Alejandro.

Once I got to the car—still there thank goodness—I sat for a couple of minutes trying to will the pain away. How the hell was I going to investigate this case? I jumped when someone knocked on my window. Alejandro. I rolled it down. He leaned in and dropped a piece of paper onto my floor.

"Boss says, 'have a nice day.'" He grinned as I rolled my window back up. As anxious as I was to read the note, I knew that I had to get out of there pretty quickly. I drove back to the "good" side of town. Found a Starbucks drive-through and got myself a Grande Caramel Macchiato. My favorite. I pulled into the parking lot and sipped at it. I bent down to retrieve the note.

Jessie was involved with someone she kept secret. Maybe he was married. He came to the club on Thursdays. Got her off drugs. She loved him. Never told me his name. Told me she was knocked up day before yesterday. I hope you find the SOB that did this to her.-Patty

Patty? Who was Patty? I pulled my notebook out of the glove box. I stashed it in there thinking I might need to consult my old notes. I flipped pages until I found what I wanted.

Patty Wilcox, one of the other girls who worked at the club. I wondered if that was the girl watching me walk in. Jessie talked to her day before yesterday? So much for Jessie staying away from stripping. I needed to talk to Patty in person. But, not today. I already did more today than I had done in months. My leg throbbed like a bad toothache.

I took another sip of my designer coffee. *Yum.* I spent the next half-hour reading through my sparse notes. I investigated Jessie's involvement with Barre as soon as I found out she was stripping. I must've talked to Patty at one time. I had no memory of her. The docs said it was expected I'd lose some of my memory after a trauma like mine. I guess I hit my head pretty hard on the concrete after I fell. My first memory was waking up in the hospital a couple of days later in pain and hooked up to tubes. I remember Cindy visiting me, Jessie, Byron, other cops from the precinct. Father Mark came bringing me bright yellow sunflowers, my favorite flower. The pain meds kept me sedated and I remember having vivid dreams. Nothing I could remember now but at the time they appeared too real. I still woke up screaming. PTSD, or post-traumatic stress-disorder, the docs called it. The captain wanted me to see the police psychologist but since I wasn't a cop anymore I didn't see the need.

I pulled an evidence bag out of my pocket and slipped the note inside of it.

I drove back to my condo on the north side of Beechton. The maple trees were in full bloom, The vivid reds, yellows and orange leaves fluttered in the slight breeze. I used to love this time of year. But, I wasn't looking forward to winter and all the snow and ice. I glanced at my cane as I drove. I hoped to be done with the cane before the bad weather hit. I couldn't see myself negotiating the icy sidewalks with a cane.

When I got closer to my condo something looked amiss. My garage door was open. I distinctly remember closing it. I fingered my side where I used to keep my gun almost without thinking. Instead of pulling into the garage I pulled into the first empty parking slot across from my garage. Should I call 911? I decided not to. I walked into the garage; since it was just me I had very little in the garage, just a few boxes and an old rusty bike I'd never ride again. There was no where anyone could hide. I went to the door that connected the condo to the garage. I left it unlocked. It was partially open. I eased it open more until it was wide enough for me to see through. I didn't see anyone. The sound of pots rattling came from the kitchen. I gulped pushing the door open wider branishing my cane as if it were a weapon.

Byron walked out from around the kitchen counter smiling at me. He wiped his hands on a towel. Relief poured through me as I put the cane against the wall.

"Oh, I didn't hear the car drive in. I left the garage open for you." I put the cane down.

"How'd you get the garage open?" I asked, making my way to the couch. I sat down trying not to moan aloud.

"You gave me a garage opener, remember?" he smiled. "Want something to drink?"

"Can't drink alcohol," I said, wondering what he was doing here. Byron noticed as I dragged my leg up onto the coffee table.

"Ice pack?" he asked.

"Sure, thanks." He brought me an ice pack and handed it to me. I stuffed it behind me. Something smelled good. I sniffed the air with appreciation. "What smells good?"

"My famous spaghetti with meatballs, garlic bread and salad with Italian dressing."

Despite my misgivings my mouth watered. "You didn't have to make me a meal," I said. He went back into the kitchen and came back with two glasses. He handed me one.

"Sparkling cranberry juice," he said, sitting next to me. I took a sip of the juice.

"Thanks, why are you here?"

He laughed. "I wanted to see you, Mel. There's enough for two if you want me to stay. If not, then you'll have enough for several days." He lay back against the cushions.

"Won't your girlfriend get mad?" I asked taking another sip.

"Which one?" he joked.

"The cop one," I said, avoiding looking at him.

"The cop one is no longer a cop but I hear she's a P.I. now."

I turned to stare at him. "Seriously, Byron? Why are you here?"

He took a sip of his drink before answering. "I haven't seen you in weeks, Mel. Every time I want to come over you have an excuse. I miss you. I miss us." He scooted closer to me, putting an arm around my shoulders. I relaxed into his embrace. It felt wonderful to have him next to me. I sighed. I missed him too. I inhaled his masculine scent mixed with his aftershave along with gun oil and grinned.

"What about your new partner?"

"Jacobs? He's not as pretty as you," Byron said. He extracted himself and went to the kitchen. I closed my eyes for a second.

He gently shook my shoulder. "Hey, sleepyhead, it's ready. Need a hand up?" I nodded. He helped me stand, handing me the cane. I stood getting my bearings. He had set the table too. I smiled. It was like old times.

"It looks good, Byron, thanks." He dished up spaghetti for me, sprinkling fresh Parmesan cheese on both the salad and the spaghetti. He poured me more sparkling juice. I took a bite of the salad. It was heavenly. I ate like I haven't eaten in days. Maybe I haven't. I had a hard time remembering.

He ate most of his salad before I finished two bites. His cell phone went off.

"Damn," he said. "I better take this." I nodded focused on my food. He went into the other room. I took a bite of the garlic bread. It was buttery and the bread melted in my mouth. Byron was a great cook. If he ever decided not to be a cop he'd make it as a chef. I smiled at my musings.

Byron came back in. He looked sheepish. "I'm sorry, Mel. I gotta go." He started picking up dishes. "I'll put these away and you'll have enough for another meal or two." He bustled around putting stuff away. I stayed in my chair. It would be too much of an effort to get up anyway. He came over and kissed my cheek.

"If you want I'll come back after my shift and bring pizza. We'll make a night of it, Mel." He nuzzled my neck. As much as I wanted him to be back in my bed I knew that he'd want more than I could give right now. Or ever. Who knows how long it's going to take me to recover? If I ever do. I didn't want to burden him with that.

"No, I have enough to eat, Byron. Take your call. I'll be fine." Both of us knew what I was saying. He withdrew. I could feel his stare behind me.

"You sure?" he asked.

"Yes," I said, staring at the salad bowl instead of Byron's face.

"See you later, Mel," he said, going out the door. I heard the garage door close. Sighing I took another forkful of salad.

***

A knock on my door woke me. Not again. I glanced at the clock on my phone. Just past midnight. I hobbled down the stairs and peered through the peephole. *Byron.* And in his hands he held a pizza box. I unchained the door, unlocked it and opened it.

"Told you I'd be back," he said, pushing past me. "I brought your favorite, mushrooms, ham and bacon." *Oh to heck with it. In for a penny, in for a pound, as my mom used to say.*

"Where's yours?" I laughed, taking the box. I started for the kitchen but he took the box back out of my hands.

"No, you go back upstairs. I'll bring us napkins, plates and something to drink." I hesitated for a nanosecond. I went back upstairs and sat cross-legged on the bed. Byron came back with the pizza, napkins, two bottles of Coke and paper plates. He began to take his shirt off.

"Wait, I thought we were having pizza," I said.

"We are, afterwards," he said smiling at me. *Oh.*

"I don't know if I can…because of my back," I said, wincing at the words. *If he expected me to be like I was before, I couldn't face it. I used to be well, flexible.* He came over to me and bent down giving me a deep kiss. I wanted him, oh, how I wanted him. But, I was afraid. He stood back up.

"Don't laugh but I found this book online and it gave me some ideas," he said.

"Really? Where is this book now? I might want to read it."

"I…er…lost it." Right. I laughed.

"I have it covered," he said. And he did. I hardly had to do any work at all. My back didn't hurt. Afterwards he fed me pizza by hand. If I was a cat I'd purr.

"Thanks for this," I said. indicating the pizza and the bed.

"I love you, Mel. I'd do anything for you. I don't want you to push me away any longer. I've given you enough time on your own. I need to be back in your life."

I nodded. "I'm in pain all the time, Byron. I don't know if I can manage anymore." I burst into tears. "I can't live like this, I want my life back." I sobbed into his shoulder. He patted my head making shushing sounds. At some point I slipped down back into the pillows. Exhausted, I finally slept.

Chapter Four

I woke to an empty bed. The pain in my leg fooled me into thinking it had left the building. When I got out of bed it reminded me I needed to take my pills. I sighed. Most of my pills were downstairs. I smelled coffee. I made my way to the bathroom and took a quick, pain-filled shower. Wincing, I wrapped up in my midnight blue fluffy robe and headed downstairs. My cane sat at the bottom of the stairs. I put my weight on it heading toward the delicious coffee smell emulating from the kitchen. I spied Byron at the stove.

"Morning," I called. My pills were on the counter. I opened several bottles upending them onto my palm. Byron smiled handing me a cup of coffee. I used it to gulp down my pills. He kissed me on the cheek. As much as I adored having him stay over last night, I savored my solitude. "Thanks," I said. His brown eyes twinkled at me.

“I made eggs and toast too,” he said. “It’s in the oven on low. Ready when you are.” He glanced at the clock on the wall. “I gotta run, Mel. See you later?” He was dressed in a dark gray suit set off by a pale blue shirt and a blue striped tie. The pale blue set off his dark colored skin nicely. I smiled. He looked good.

“Sure, breakfast smells good. Appreciate it.” I sat down in the nearest kitchen chair with a grimace. He noticed.

“Pain today?” he asked.

“Always,” I said taking another swallow of my coffee.

“Heard you paid a visit to Barre yesterday,” he said, giving me a look as he straightened his tie.

“Who told you that?” I asked.

“A little birdie named Alejandro.”

“You talked to him?” I asked.

He shook his head. “Let’s say that I persuaded him to tell me all he knows about Barre Enterprises.” I smiled.

"He sang like a canary?" It was one of our private jokes. He whistled a tune trying to sound bird-like. I laughed. "Learn anything new?"

"Not really, nothing except a certain P.I. named Thompson came to visit and got a note from a certain stripper named Patty." He held out his hand to me. "Hand it over, Mel." I indicated my bag hanging on a hook by the door.

"It's in there in an evidence bag. I handled it a bit."

He rummaged in the bag pulling out the note I had put in an evidence bag. He raised his eyebrows at the plastic bag.

"Where'd you get these? Steal them?" As if I would admit that. I shook my head.

"Bought them off the Internet, 100 in a pack." He tucked the bag into his pocket. I indicated the clock. "Thought you had to run?"

"I'm going soon. I want you to stay out of this, Mel. Barre is bad news. He had you shot. I can't prove it but you and I know he orchestrated it. Leave him alone before he hurts you again."

"I can't," I said. It was hard to stare him down when he was hovering by the door and I was in a chair too paralyzed with pain to move. "I have a client."

"Who? Cindy?"

"Client privilege. Can't say," I said.

"The M.E. ruled it a suicide. Tell Cindy her daughter jumped because she was involved with some bad dudes."

"Seriously? That's what I'm supposed to tell the mother of a dead girl? Oh, sorry your daughter is dead but that's what happens when you are with 'bad dudes'?"

"Mel," his voice took on the quality I named the, Mel-You-Better-F-Off-Or-Else quality.

I was too weary to deal with him this morning. I stretched out my bad leg.

"Go to work, Byron. I've got it covered," I said copying him.

"You don't even have a gun anymore," he said. He had a point there. I needed to get a gun, and fast. He walked back over to me. "At least promise me you'll be careful and no more dealings with Barre or his crew."

"You know I can't promise that," I said, finishing up the coffee. I showed him the empty mug. "Any more coffee?"

"I made a pot, couldn't figure out that new one. Found the old one in the closet." He leaned down nuzzling my neck again. I sighed with contentment. "I'll miss you P.I. Thompson," he said. This time he left. He shut the door behind him then yelled, "Lock it." I laughed.

I sat where I was until the smell of the plate in the oven wafted over to me. I got up to get an oven mitt forgetting about my leg and crashed to the dining room floor.

"Damn it," I screamed, more angry than hurt. I scooted over to the chair to pull myself up to a standing position. Leaning on my cane I made my way to the kitchen.

Breakfast was delicious even though the eggs were dried out by the time I ate them. I preferred mine swimming in ketchup with a dash of hot sauce.

The phone rang just as I was pulling on my jeans. Cindy's face came up on the screen. It was either one of Cindy's kids or Cindy herself. I answered knowing full well I'd regret it.

"Hello?"

"Mel? Any luck yet?" It's been, what? A day and some change? No luck except I almost got beat up by some thugs, fell down twice, let my cop boyfriend back into my bed and now he wants to move back in, and got a note from a stripper who may know nothing about Jessie's boyfriend but definitely knew she was pregnant. That was one bit of news I wasn't going to share with Cindy at the moment.

"Not yet." I sat down heavily on the bed. My cane just out of reach. I eyed it with disdain. Why did the stupid thing fly over to me like things did in the Harry Potter movies?
"Did the kids get there okay?"

"Yes, John is arranging everything. He's having a memorial for Jessie on Saturday. We decided to have her cremated. The funeral home is picking her up tomorrow." Cremated? There goes any evidence up in smoke. I shook my head then realized she couldn't see me.

"I think you should wait on that, Cindy."

"Why?"

"Uh…in case of new evidence showing up. If she's cremated we won't have any proof of anything."

"I hadn't thought of that. I'll have John call the funeral home and we'll do a closed casket instead. I have a picture of Jessie when she was in *Les Misérables* in high school I can ask Joan to enlarge it and we'll display it at the front of the church. Thanks for all your help on this, Mel. I know in my heart that my Jessie would never kill herself, no matter what." I heard other family members say that to me and usually blew them off. But this time I agreed with Cindy. There was something hinky about this. If Jessie was pregnant, why would she kill herself? From the time she was little she talked about having her own family. Plus she was Catholic. Or had been at one time. She'd have that baby no matter what.

"Look, Cindy. Do you have the key to Jessie's apartment?"

"I gave it to Bryon. He came by this morning and asked me for it. Said they wanted to tie up loose ends." I couldn't help but smile at this good news. This meant that Byron believed me. He was investigating on his own.

"Thanks, Cindy. I gotta go. I'll try and catch Byron before he leaves. Oh, call me with the memorial details."

Moving at my usual snail's pace I made it over to Jessie's apartment in less than thirty minutes. My pain pills were on board so I was in minimal pain. I glanced at the driveway as I pulled up. Jessie's car was gone, I wondered if the police impounded it. Byron's gray Honda Accord was still parked there. I pulled in behind it. When I got to the door Byron yanked it open.

"I'd ask what you are doing here, Thompson but why bother?" He wasn't mad just exasperated. I shrugged as I went inside. The place was neat and clean. Too clean. I looked at Byron.

"Did you dust for prints?"

"What for? I told you it's been ruled a suicide."

"Why are you here?" I raised my eyebrows at him. He smirked at me running a hand over his bald head. He shaved it every morning. I often wondered if he did to look more imposing than his five foot nine slight frame allowed him to look.

"For the same reason you are," he said. He touched his middle. "I have a gut feeling that this is not suicide. Can't quite figure it out yet though."

"Find anything?"

"Not really. Her laptop is clean. No incriminating entries in her online blog. The only thing she said was that she was in love but didn't give any names or even initials." He sighed.

"Did you make copies of her blog?" I asked. He nodded. "What about her cell phone?"

"It's in a million pieces in the evidence room, she had it in her pocket when she fell."

"I just don't believe she'd kill herself even if she was pregnant," I said. Byron did one of those double takes they do on TV, impressive.

"How'd you know that?" he asked. "It wasn't released to the press."

"Patty wrote it to me in that note. Didn't you read it?" I asked.

"Not yet." He dug it out of his pocket where he had stashed it. He read it through the plastic then tucked it back in his pocket. "Interesting." I could almost hear the wheels and clicks as he thought about this new evidence.

"Reopen as a murder case?" I asked.

"Not yet. M.E. thinks she was about eight weeks along, too soon to be showing. She decided to off herself by diving off the tallest building she could find before her mom or the boyfriend found out. He is probably married."

"No," I shook my head. "You met Jessie, she was a happy kid. Even with the stripping and the drugs, I doubt she'd do this, Byron. She loved life."

"Even those of us that love it can get tired of it," he said.

My stomach sank. Did he mean me? There were days when I wish I could travel back in time before all this happened and yeah, I had my days spent in bed crying. A pity party attended by me. But, those days were getting fewer and fewer apart. I felt stronger emotionally. But being at Jessie's didn't make me feel any stronger. I spied the Hello Kitty duffel bag I had given her at her high school graduation sitting in the corner of the room. A sob escaped before I could stop it.

"What's wrong?" Byron asked staring at me. I pointed to the duffel bag.

"I gave that to Jessie at her graduation. It was a running joke with us. She used to be into Hello Kitty and I bought her everything with Hello Kitty on it. Cindy even had her room decorated with Hello Kitty stuff." I hesitated. "I think she was nine. Anyway, as she got older and stopped liking Hello Kitty I continued the tradition. Every time she had a birthday or event I bought her something with Hello Kitty on it."

"You can probably take it, I'm sure Cindy would let you have it."

I shook my head. "No, it would remind me of her too much." On an impulse I went over to the bag. I rummaged around inside. I found an entire change of clothes, including clean underwear and a toothbrush. "She must've used this as an overnight bag."

"Too bad we didn't know who she was overnighting with," Byron said. A knock on the door interrupted us.

An older lady with tight gray pin curls and a pair of pink eyeglasses dangling on a gold chain around her neck stuck her head in the door. "Excuse me?" she said, coming further in. She had on one of those dresses they used to call mu-mu's. This one had large purple and yellow flowers all over it. On her feet were a pair of bright pink slippers. She beamed at us.

"I'm Mrs. Forest? I'm the landlady. I'm so sorry to hear about Miss Lewis. I read it in the paper and Muffy and I cried and cried."

"Muffy?" I asked.

"My Pom. Pomeranian. She's the color of the carpet. So sweet too. Just like Miss Lewis." Both Byron and I looked down at the carpet. It was a hideous shade of beige. "Anywho, Miss Lewis was infested with ants and the exterminator is here so would it be okay to let him in? I want to rent the apartment again soon." She looked expectantly at us. "Do either of you know when I can rent it out again? I have to contact the family to have them clean it out. The rent is paid up until the end of the month."

"We'll let you know," Byron said. "Someone will probably come back at a later time to talk to you, Mrs. Forest. Were you the only one that had a key to Jessie's…er…Miss Lewis' apartment?"

"I believe so. She never asked me for a second key. She was a good tenant. Quiet as a church mouse. Worked the late shift so she slept during the day. I will have to change the locks now I suppose." She nodded to herself as she shuffled out to the curb where an exterminator truck sat.

"You sure it's okay to let the exterminator in?" I asked.

"Even if it does turn out she was murdered, she wasn't killed here. We'll go through her apartment with that in mind at a later date."

"Well, I guess our next stop is to see Stripper Patty."

"Our next stop?" Now it was his turn to raise his eyebrows. "Mel, you know I can't take you with me on an ongoing investigation."

"Ah, but this is not an ongoing investigation, remember?" He sighed. "What does Jacobs think about all this?" We were walking toward my car.

"He thinks I'm an idiot. And that I let my ba…er…that I left my brains in my pants."

I laughed. "He sounds fun," I said with a sarcastic tone. I stood up. "Let's go see Patty."

"You doin' okay, Thompson?" His brown eyes were full of concern.

"I am right now, Williams. That's why we have to hustle. Never know when the pain meds are gonna leave." I smiled at him. "Oh, by the way, I parked behind you so I better drive."

If there was one thing that Byron hated above all others, it was letting someone else drive. And he despised the color of my car, told me he felt like he was riding around in a neon sign. He fumed but got into the passenger side without complaint. I turned my head so he wouldn't see my half smile.

"I'm assuming you have Patty's address?" I asked. He recited it.

Patty lived in a modest house on a quiet street. A knock at the door brought a small tow-headed child peering at us. A voice from the other room said,

"How many times do I have to tell you not to open that door whenever someone knocks?" The voice belonged to Patty. She strode up to the door taking the boy by the hand. She grinned down at him and tousled his hair. The boy continued to peer at us."My sister's kid, I watch him during the day while she works. Help you?" She looked at Byron first, then me. Byron brought out his badge but she waved it away.

"I know who you are, come on in, please." She held the door wider so the two of us could come in. I left my cane in the car on purpose. I used the table by the door to support myself as I walked in. I plopped into the nearest chair. Byron took the chair next to me. The living room was sparsely furnished but the furniture looked lived in. I disliked those living rooms that looked as if no one was allowed to be on the furniture. I preferred a few scratches and dents to new. My leg ached. I rubbed my thigh. Patty noticed.

"I saw you the other day at Barre's with your cane." She perched on the edge of a hard-backed chair that she brought in from the kitchen. The boy settled into her lap. He looked at us with wide eyes. She jostled him but he squirmed down onto the floor. He began playing with a toy truck making varoom noises. Patty stared down at him. "Luke? Auntie Patty wants you to go play in your room while she talks to these nice people, okay?" He clutched the truck to his chest and walked silently away. She sighed. She hitched up her dark green skirt so that more of her legs showed. I guess for Byron's sake. She faced him twirling a yellow strand of hair around and around a finger. I swear if she giggled I was going to smack her one. The green sweater she wore—to match her skirt no doubt—looked a couple of sizes too small. She arched her back so that her breasts were more prominent. I wondered if this was a ruse to get Byron's mind off whatever it was she thought he was going to ask or if it was one of her natural ways of posturing whenever a male was around. I briefly glanced down at my too big tee shirt. It wouldn't matter how much I arched my back—not that I would because pain would ensue if I did—my breasts would never look any bigger. I glanced back up to see both Byron and Patty's eyes on me.

"What?" I asked.

"Patty asked what you wanted to know about Jessie," Byron said. He turned so that he was angled toward me, not Patty. I relaxed.

"Uh, tell me everything. How you met, just give me the bullet points." Byron winced at those words.

"Sure." She crossed and uncrossed her long legs, wiggling her bare toes. "Jessie and I met at the club. She was nervous at first but she got the hang of it real fast." Patty looked around the room. "Mind if I smoke? I'm dying for a cigarette. Grace won't let me smoke in here but I do it all the time," she grinned. "That's what air fresheners are for."

She got up and took out a pack of cigarettes from a bag lying on the floor near the couch. From here I could see the contents quite clearly. I saw the fixings for cooking something hard, heroin or cocaine and the thing that interested me the most, a gun. I glanced at Byron but his sight line didn't allow him to see the bag. Patty saw me looking and drew it closed with a drawstring. I didn't say anything. Before she sat down she gestured to the back of the house. "I gotta check on Luke. He just ate lunch and needs to take a nap." The two of us nodded. It was a perfect opportunity for me to tell Byron about the drug paraphernalia and the gun. I kept quiet. I wanted to find out more first. I figured if I told on her she'd close down. I needed to know what she knew. *Sorry, Byron*. Patty returned in a couple of minutes. "He fell asleep on the floor, poor guy." She sat back down and lit a cigarette. She indicated the pack to me, then to Byron. "Want one?" Both of us shook our heads. Byron got out a notepad.

"Tell us about Jessie. When did you see her last?" he asked.

"Well, let me think." She inhaled then blew out smoke, in my direction I might add. I coughed discretely. She jiggled one foot over the other. I studied her facial features. She looked too pretty. She had on minimal makeup but even with it on she looked like she could be an actress or model. What had happened to her? How did she end up as a stripper with a gun and drugs in her bag? I tuned in to what she was saying.

"I saw Jessie on Monday; no it must've been Sunday night late. She called me crying that the guy she was involved with didn't want her to have the baby. He wanted her to get rid of it and he wanted her to leave town. He offered her money but she refused to take it. She wanted to raise the baby as a single mom. He told her that it would be impossible to do that in Beechton and she'd have to go away to a big city like New York or LA.I figured he was a bigwig. Maybe the mayor." Patty smoked in silence for a time."I had just finished a shift so I was beat. I told her to call me back in the morning and we'd figure it out." She sighed. "I never heard from her again. I read it in the paper the next day. Poor lamb."

"And you have no idea who this mystery man is?" I asked. She waved her cigarette around dropping ash on the beige carpet.

"No, no clue. I know she met him right after you read her the riot act and he got her clean. He came to the club on Thursdays at first then he stopped coming after Jessie quit. And before you ask, Thursday is my night off so I have no idea what he looked like."

"So, you never met this guy?" Byron asked.

"I didn't pry, ya know? To each his own. We were work friends but we didn't socialize after work."

"So, you don't know if this guy was married or not?" She shook her head staring at Byron then looked at me.

"I heard that Barre was pissed that you made Jessie quit."

"Yeah, I heard that too," I said, stretching out my left leg. She nodded.

"I don't suppose you know anything about that," Byron asked. She shook her head again.

"Nope, sorry." Just then the front door opened and a woman who looked like an older version of Patty came in. She was shorter and rounder but had the same blonde hair and high cheekbones. Her blue eyes matched Patty's. She carried two grocery bags in her arms. Byron—ever the gentleman—jumped up to help her.

"Who are these people, Patty? And I thought I told you, no smoking around Luke! Where is he?"

"He's taking a nap, give it a rest, Gracie. These are cops."

"Cops? What'd you do now?" Her eyes slid to Byron. "The kitchen is through here." Byron grinned at me as he followed her with the bags in his arms.

"Gracie is on the straight and narrow, me? Not so much." Patty laughed putting out the cigarette in a saucer. She looked expectantly at me.

"Look, I'd tell you more if I knew more. I don't. I liked Jessie. She was fun. You know we made those movies together?"

"I saw them."

"What'd ya think?" She fluffed her long curly hair as if she was primping for the camera. Ready for my close up Mr. Deville.

"I don't remember much except a lot of heaving bodies and moaning," I said. She nodded.

"But the moaning sounded real, right?"She let her gaze drift to the window. "You know that classic scene in Harry and Sally when she pretends to come over her salad? Jessie and I did that at a restaurant once. It was hilarious. We wanted to practice so it would sound real on camera." She moved her eyes to me. "See what I mean? Fun."

"She wasn't at college on Sunday night I'm guessing," I said. Patty ran a hand through her curls musing them in an attractive way. She wrinkled her pert nose.

"Guess not, maybe she was staying with the dude that knocked her up."

"Could it have been Barre or one of his bouncers?" She laughed so hard she nearly fell off the chair.

"No, he only hires gay guys to be bouncers just for that reason."

"Is Barre gay?" She shrugged.

"Dunno. Maybe. He stays in his office mostly. Haven't seen him with anyone in particular. He always grabs us girls though, so maybe not. I heard he has problems in that area, if you know what I mean. Even the little blue pill can't help him."

Byron came back into the room. "I straightened it all out with your sister, Patty. She knows you aren't in trouble." He held out his hand to her. She got up off the chair. In her bare feet she towered over him. She glanced down at him and smiled.

"Thanks, ever fantasize about doing it with tall women?" she asked, making her voice husky.

"No, only short, gimpy ones," he joked holding out an elbow for me. I took it. He handed Patty a card. "Call me if you think of anything, Miss Wilcox." Her eyes misted over.

"No one calls me Miss Wilcox anymore." She jerked her head toward the hallway. "He's mine ya know. Looks just like me when I was his age. Gracie agreed to raise him for me. I give her money. That's funny, huh? The babysitter giving money instead of the other way 'round?" She wiped a hand across her eyes. She looked at Byron's card, licked her lips with a slow tongue then tucked the card between her breasts. "I'll call you sometime, Detective Byron. If you come into Barre's on Saturday night I'll give you a free lap dance. Promise." She bent down and kissed the top of his head. He blushed. I laughed.

"Do you think any of the girls who work on Thursday might talk to us?" I asked. Or, specifically to me.

"I doubt it, Barre has us on a tight leash, one slip up, like talking to the cops and you are gone for good." She snapped her fingers. I wasn't sure if she meant fired or dead.

"And you aren't worried about talking to us?" Bryon asked.

She tossed her hair again. "She was my friend. I wanna help. My sister is gonna pay for me to go to community college so I can get out of exotic dancing." She winked at Bryon. He stood.

This time I handed her my business card fresh from the online site I used. "If any of the others know anything, give me a call." She gazed at my card.

"A P.I.? I thought you were a cop," she said.

"I was, now I'm not."

Once we were in the car and a couple of blocks away I told Byron about the drug stuff and the gun.

"I'm not in narcotics and the gun is probably for protection."

"Probably. I'm sorry I didn't tell you right away but I didn't want her to shut down on us." He nodded. "We need to find this mysterious boyfriend of Jessie's."

"I agree but our leads are dwindling."

"Has that ever stopped us before?" I asked turning onto the street where the precinct was located. I pulled up in front. Byron put his hand on the door.

"I want you to go home and rest, Mel. I'll catch a ride back to Jessie's apartment to pick up my car with Jacobs." I pointed out the door. A big beefy cop was striding toward us and he didn't look happy.

"That him?" Byron shut his eyes for a moment.

"Yep." He jumped out of the car before Jacobs came up to it. "I'm here, Jacobs, what's the emergency?"

"The Loo has a bee up his you know what. Said he was tryin' to reach you all night. Where ya been?" He glanced in the car at me. I wiggled fingers at him. He smirked. "Better get your butt in there pronto. Next time answer your cell or he'll have my head."

Byron leaned in before shutting the car door. "I better see what the Loo wants, I'll see you later."

Chapter Five

Just as I was about to put the car in gear my phone rang. I glanced at the number. ST. MATTHEW'S.

"Hello?"

"Mel? This is Father Mark at St. Matt's, how are you doing?"

"Father Mark! It's so good to hear your voice. I'm hanging in there. What's up?"

"Cindy Lewis has asked me to officiate at the memorial for Jessie on Saturday. She said you are investigating Jessie's death."

"Yes, I am." I guess if Cindy already told him it was okay to validate it. Why was he calling me? Did he hope to dig up all the sordid details for the church bulletin?

"Find anything yet?"

"Not yet. Look, I'm kinda busy, why did you call exactly?" I figured that seven circles of Hell waited for me because I was rude to a priest but I couldn't drive and talk at the same time. I wasn't that talented.

"I just wanted you to know the memorial starts at 11 and we will be serving a buffet afterwards provided by the Ladies Auxiliary." *Yum.* Their foods always contained butter, lard, more butter and oh, lard. I shuddered slightly.

"Thanks for the info, Father. I'll see you on Saturday."

"I was wondering…" Here it comes. The real reason he called.

"Yes?"

"As you know Jessie cannot be buried on church ground if she killed herself. That's why it's imperative you let me know if she didn't commit suicide." Right. I forgot about that little glitch in the Catholic Church. Hallowed ground and all that.

"There's nothing official yet, Father. But, I can tell you that I am investigating with that idea in mind."

"Yes, I thought you might be." He paused clearing his throat. "Jessie was a troubled girl.

She came to me several months ago and confessed she was taking drugs, working at that strip club and letting men and women do all sorts of depraved acts to her body. She hated all of it." He hesitated again. "She even made two of those, what do you call them? Promo movies?"

"Porno movies, Father."

"Right, porno movies. She had intercourse on film with a woman and with a man, at the same time."

"I know, I saw them." Silence on the other end. "No, not that way. When I was trying to help her, before I got shot. When I was still a cop." As if that made a difference. Maybe it did.

"They paid her a lot of money, most of it went to her college tuition. She called it her 'blood money.'"

"I'm sure they did. What did you say to her when she came to you?"

"I can't reveal anything said to me in the confessional, Mel. You know that." I did.

"Even if that person is now dead?"

"Yes. The Seal of the Confessional cannot be broken for any reason." I waited a beat.

"I better go, Father. I'll see you on Saturday."

"Fine. Could you make sure to sit up front with Cindy and her remaining children?"

"Yes, of course."

"I may call on you to offer your thoughts and memories of Jessie." I knew it. This was the real reason he called.

"I don't do well with crowds, Father."

"This is for Jessie and for her family and friends."

I sighed. "Fine. But it'll have to be short."

"Whatever you come up with will be appropriate, I'm sure. Goodbye, Mel. Don't make us wait so long before we see you again." I hung up without saying goodbye. Seven circles. of Hell.

* * *

We cuddled on the couch after Byron brought us Chinese take-out for dinner. He even remembered chopsticks for me. Today was one of my good days. The pain at a minimum. My kind of day. We went over the notes from Patty's conversation. Neither one of us could see a connection or a pattern. I wondered about Barre some more. I knew he was involved but, how?

"Hey, why does Jacobs hate me so much?" I asked, popping a bamboo shoot in my mouth. Moo Goo Gai Pan was one of my favorite Chinese dishes.

"He thinks you are corrupting me and since you are no longer a cop, he doesn't trust you."

"He doesn't even know me," I said. I speared a piece of chicken from his General Tso Chicken dish and chewed it slowly. "This is spicy but good," I said, spearing another piece.

He waved my chopstick away with a hand as I attempted to spear a third piece. "Eat your own," he said, laughing. I hadn't felt this relaxed in months. I leaned into Byron's shoulder. "Hey, Mel. Can I ask you something?"

I felt sleepy from all the food. "Sure," I mumbled. "What?"

"Can I move back in? You know, with my own drawer and everything?"

I sat up suddenly more awake. "Move in?" I croaked. *Damn, just when everything was going so well.* He studied my face then began to stack the food cartons into piles.

"I guess I got my answer." He got up to go to the kitchen.

"No, Byron, don't go. It's just that you sprung it on me. Give me some time to think about it, please?"

"Either you want me here all the time, or you don't. If you don't that's fine. I'll come over once a week so we can have a night of fun and then go on my merry way." His feelings were hurt. I sighed. I didn't do well with feelings.

"Byron, it's just that getting shot has changed me."

"And you no longer want me in your house?" His back was to me.

"No, that's not what I meant. It's that I…" Oh, hell, what was I saying? I wanted him in my bed but not in my house? That wasn't fair to him or to me. What the hell did I want? I had no clue. "Okay, you can move in," I said with a smile. He whipped around staring at me.

"Now you are patronizing me, Mel. No, thanks. I don't want your pity. Poor Byron, all alone."

"That's not what I meant, Byron. Please? Move back in?"

He shook his head at me. His eyes sad."No, I don't think so. I won't ask again, Mel. Maybe it's time for both of us to move on."

Move on? What did he mean, move on? I tell him I want to think about it and he tells me it's over? I blinked back tears of anger.

"Fine, move on. Maybe you could give Patty a call, I'm sure she'd be interested." I sank back against the couch cushions. Let him go if he wants to go. The problem was, I didn't want him to leave. *Now, you figure it out Thompson? You are a complete idiot.*

He stared at me. "Maybe I will take her up on that free lap dance."

"Yeah, kinda hard for me to lap dance with a gimp leg," I snarled. For some reason this struck both of us as funny. We burst out laughing. Byron sat down next to me caressing my good leg.

"I love you, Mel. You know I do. I want us to be together but, if it isn't something you want, then it won't work."

I sighed again. "Can you give me some time to figure this all out, Byron? Please?"

"If you are worried I'll love you less because of your leg, I won't." He smiled.

"I know. You are much more kind-hearted than I'll ever be."

"Yeah, God forbid if I ever got shot and had a permanent injury, you'd be out the door in two seconds flat."

"Or less," I said, smiling.

He gathered me in his arms. "Tabled for tonight," he said, kissing me. "But soon, it has to be all or nothing, Mel. I'm too old to live like a bachelor crashing on Jacob's floor."

"Oh, so that's why you want to move back in?"

"Yeah, plus he snores." Needless to say we didn't even make it upstairs. Byron made it work even without the lap dance.

Chapter Six

Saturday was one of those clear autumn days that made you think winter would never come. Sunny, bright blue skies greeted me as I stumbled out of bed. I decided against a shower. As I limped over to get my pain pills off the dresser my leg began to scream at me. I hobbled back to the bed, pills in hand and a water bottle on my nightstand. I downed the pills with a swallow of water. *Jesus, this hurts.* I massaged the leg hoping that would make it feel better. Not that I haven't tried that before. I stretched it out on the bed. Nope. I needed an ice pack. Downstairs. I sighed grabbing the cane from beside the bed. I cursed all the way down the stairs. I grabbed an ice pack and put it on my leg. I sat at my computer. Opening up a word document I made a list of all of the possibilities. Just like I'd do if I were still a cop and investigating her murder. The list was shorter than I liked

.

Patty

unknown possibly married guy

Barre

Alejandro

Sven

Grace-Patty's sister

some other person as yet unknown

I got up and brewed myself a cup of French Roast and popped a bagel in the toaster. I sat back down until the bagel came up. I buttered it, took my coffee and sat in the chair mulling over the situation. Why did Jessie jump off the building? Was she upset about her pregnancy? It didn't sound like it. I wish I knew more of her friends. She had to confide in someone, but, who? I gave up waiting for the pain pills to work. I had to get dressed for the memorial. I slipped on a pair of black slacks, a navy blouse with a navy blazer over it. I slid my feet into black ballet flats. I combed my hair, fluffed it with my fingers and I was ready to go out the door. I glanced at my image in the bathroom mirror. I still looked like a cop. I narrowed my eyes like I used to do with suspects. Fierce. I gathered my bag and my cane before heading to the garage.

Parking attendants motioned me to the next open parking space. The church parking lot was almost full to capacity. I didn't know Jessie knew so many people. Maybe some of them were friends of Cindy. I walked up to the church steps. Grimacing, I managed to go up several without stopping. At the top of the steps Father Mark himself stood there greeting people.

He took both my hands in his. "Mel, so glad you are here. Cindy has been asking about you." He bent down and kissed my cheek. "It's a sad day for all of us. Call my secretary this week, I'd love to have you come for dinner." Father Mark and I used to have a monthly dinner before I got shot. I haven't been to his house since then. "I've got some new pieces to show you." Father Mark did wood carving in his spare time. He was very gifted. I still had the tiny horse he carved for me when I graduated the police academy. He dropped my hands to greet the next person coming up the stairs. I took that as my clue to move on. I spotted a chair in the foyer. I made a bee-line for it. Once I was sitting, I took some deep breaths. How was I going to get through this day? My leg tingled and ached. It felt like someone was stabbing the side of my leg with a hot poker and a sharp knife all at the same time. I lay the cane against the side of the chair. I took another deep breath and laid my head back closing my eyes. I was willing the pain to go away. Of course the pain never listened. A hand on my knee made me start. I opened my eyes. *Byron.*

"You okay, Mel? You look a little pale."

"I'm fine, the walk from the parking lot was longer than I expected. I'll be okay in a couple of minutes." Byron cleaned up nicely. He had on a dark blue suit, a cream colored shirt under the jacket with a yellow and blue striped tie. I nodded. "You look good," I said.

"You too. Want a hand up?" We both heard the music starting. I nodded. He helped me up, handed me the cane and the two of us walked to the front of the church. I sat down next to Cindy and Byron sat down next to me. I waved at John, on Cindy's other side and Joan who ignored me.

"Where's Joey?" I stage-whispered to Cindy.

She shook her head, tears beginning to form. "He stayed in San Francisco. Said he couldn't make it," Cindy said.

"He just didn't want to show his face around here," John said in a louder voice. "Thanks for coming, Mel."

"Why? What happened with Joey?" I asked also too loud. People stared at us.

"Jessie called him and asked if she could fly out to be with him and his boyfriend and he said no," John said with a sneer. John was not gay-friendly. As the eldest he took it upon himself to run the family when their dad died. Joey came out to them last Christmas. The only thing John said was that he was glad his dad wasn't there to witness Joey's coming out. Joey, hurt and abandoned fled back to San Francisco. He got a job and a boyfriend and hasn't been home since. Not that I blamed him. I would've liked to have seen him though. I mused about what John said. I'd call Joey when I got back. I stuck my leg out trying to ease the tingling/burning. I needed my ice pack. I shifted in my seat. Byron put a hand on my knee.

"Hang in there, Mel. If you need to leave, just go." I nodded. I had no intention of leaving. I turned around scanning the now-filled church. Plenty of faces I didn't know stared back at me. Patty waved to me. She had her little boy with her. Some of the other girls from Barre—I recognized a few of them—sat near Patty. Barre wasn't in attendance, not that I could see him anyway and neither were the bouncer twins. I knew that Jessie's married boyfriend would be here but which one was he? Was he that guy in the back pew all by himself? His eyes shifted back and forth as he watched the crowd as if he was afraid someone would recognize him. Or was it the guy in the middle pew with the wife and kiddies? He smiled at me and I looked away. I turned back as Father Mark stood in front of the lectern to address the crowd.

"Family and friends, we are here today to celebrate the life of, Jessie Lewis, 20 year old college student, cut down in the prime of life by unknown persons." The crowd started mumbling. Cindy looked at me. So did Byron.

"What did you tell him?" he whispered.

"Nothing, just that I was investigating."

"Shush," a woman with a black veiled hat on leaned over to me putting her index finger to her lips.

"Sorry," I mumbled. I looked at Father Mark. He was looking at me too. "What?" I mouthed. He gestured to the microphone.

"And now a good friend of the family, Ms. Mel Thompson will share her memories of Jessie with us." He stepped back from the microphone. I stood on shaky legs. I didn't know there would be this many people. I hated crowds.

"You don't have to do this," Byron said, handing me my cane. I nodded. Of course I did. Cindy was my best friend. I made my way to the lectern. I cleared my throat. My leg throbbed incessantly.

"Good morning. I'm Mel Thompson and I've known Jessie all her life. I was there when Jessie was born. Her mother, Cindy Lewis and I went to college together. We are best friends. I was supposed to bring the camera to record Jessie's birth, except I got so caught up in the moment when I got the call that Cindy had gone into labor that I didn't bring the camera. Cindy had the hospital photographer take extra pictures for me though." I pulled my wallet out of my front pocket and opened it. I showed the audience a picture. "Here she is, just minutes after she was born." I put the wallet back. "My favorite memory of Jessie is when she was eight. I took her to the library, not the branch one but the downtown one. When we walked in the door, she stopped. Her eyes wide. I asked her what was wrong and she said, 'Aunt Mel, is this wonderland?' I half expected to see a white rabbit hopping past us." The crowd laughed politely. "She never got over her love of books that's why all of us, including her family were so surprised when she announced at the age of 13 that she wanted to be 'an actress or a model.'" I teared up a little. "All the way through high school she acted in all the plays, worked backstage as crew and sang in the choir. She landed the lead in whatever musical the high school was doing. The senior musical was her favorite by far. She played the role of Fantine well." I pointed to the photo of her in *Les Misérables* in front of the lectern. "She was thrilled to get into State and was majoring in musical theater. She wanted to go to New York City after graduation and audition for Broadway musicals." I smiled at the memory. Here I looked at Cindy. "But, life got in the way and she had to drop down to part-time. She would've been a junior this year." I scanned the crowd. Many young college-aged students stared back at me. "She adored college and was looking to put her life back together. Too bad she never had a chance." I nodded at Father Mark who gave me a hand down the steps. I didn't sit down but kept on going down the center aisle. Once I was out the door, I limped towards the ladies room. I pushed the door open and went inside. I sat down on a faux-velvet couch and cried. I cried for Jessie, for Cindy, for Joan, Joey and John, and a little for myself. Tears spent, I got up to wash my face. I used the water from the tap to take another pain pill. I lay down on the couch in order to stretch my leg out. I heard the door open and close several times but didn't open my eyes. I dozed off. Someone shook my shoulder. Hard.

"Mel? Are you all right?" I opened my eyes. Cindy's brown eyes stared at me with concern. Her usually neat brown bun bounced at the nape of her neck and tendrils of hair escaped dangling on both sides of her face. She looked harried. She had worn a beige-colored skirt and jacket with a cream-colored blouse under the jacket. I half sat up on one elbow.

"I'm okay, just tired. The pain pills knock me out. Did I miss the memorial?"

She smiled. "Pretty much all of it. John wants to talk to you, so does Byron." I nodded. She sat down next to me and eased off both shoes wriggling her toes. "Ah, that feels good. These shoes pinch." I noticed she had on one inch pumps, also cream-colored. I put an arm around her.

"Jessie will be missed," I said. She laid her head on my shoulder.

"The worse part will be holidays. I'm so used to the kids gathering at my house. I guess it'll just be me and John and Joanie. Joey refuses to come home if John is still here."

"I'll be there, Cindy."

She started crying softly."I thought I lost you, too." I knew she was talking not only about Jessie but about her husband dying.

"You'll never lose me, Lewis. I'm stuck to you like white on rice," I chuckled.

"What does that mean exactly?" she asked getting up to splash water on her face.

"I have no idea." I got up and made my way back out into the foyer. Byron waited by the doorway, John paced the floor. Other people stood in groups quietly talking. John saw me first he came over to me taking my arm and steering me further from the crowd.

"Look, Mel. Did you find anything about Jessie's death? Anything incriminating?"

"I better talk to all of you at the same time," I said, trying to hedge.

"Tell me now, Mel. If it's important, as the delegated spokesperson for the family, I can decide if it's something they need to hear or not." I thought for a moment. He wasn't part of my suspect list. But, maybe he should be? What if he found out about Jessie's porno flick and her drug use? What if he didn't want the town to find out about her foray into the adult film industry? In this place your social standing counted for a lot. I never had any to begin with so I was in no danger of losing mine. *Fine.* I sighed again.

The M.E. said she was about eight weeks pregnant when she jumped."

"Pregnant? Oh, this is going to upset mom."

"What about you, John? Where were you when Jessie was killed?"

He shook his head."You aren't serious? I didn't kill her, I loved her. I'm her brother."

"Step-brother," I reminded him. Jessie was the only child of Cindy and Justin, her second husband. John, Joey and Joan were the offspring of Captain AJ Tanner who divorced Cindy and ran off with a waitress he met in a bar. The kids saw him a fair amount growing up. I never liked him, he believed in the 'spare the rod, spoil the child' method of child rearing. I was happy when Cindy met Justin Lewis and even happier when she found out she was pregnant with Jessie. How did life get so complicated?

"She was like a true sister to me. I never thought of her as a step-sister."

"You were only seven years old when she was born," I said, leaning on my cane for support. Byron watched me from the other side of the room. His presence comforted me.

"So?"

"So, maybe you were so jealous of her, you resented her all this time. Maybe she came to you to tell you she was pregnant with her married boyfriend's baby. I mean, it was bad enough she was into stripping, then porn, then drugs. But, a baby by a prominent figure in our town? Maybe someone you know?"

He sighed. "I haven't spoken to Jessie in months. I gave up on her when she started working at that club. I didn't know she was having an affair with a married man, who was it?"

I shrugged. "If I knew I'd already have a suspect in jail." So he already knew about the porno films. Interesting. And the drugs and the stripping. But not much got past him, he had his finger in all the pies in Beechton, maybe even The Barre.

"Want me to tell mom about Jessie?" he asked.

I shook my head."No, I'll do it. Gather everyone together at the house. I'll be over by four." He nodded. After John left, Byron came over to me.

"Feeling better after your nap?" he asked.

"How'd you know?"

"Peeked in when you didn't come out. You were out like the proverbial light. I thought I'd let you sleep."

"Guess I missed the buffet, huh?"

"You hungry?" Byron asked.

"Starved."

He held out an elbow to me. "Your chariot awaits, madam," he joked. I smiled. Cindy chose that moment to come out of the ladies room, her makeup intact and her bun fixed. She looked better.

I smiled at her. "Byron and I are going to eat something. We'll be by your place after."

She nodded biting her lower lip. "I'll see you there, Mel." She looked like she was heading somewhere.

Father Mark was once again at the doorway telling people goodbye.

"Mel, are you all right now?" he asked taking both my hands in his.

"Much better, thanks, Father."

"Take good care of this one," Father Mark said to Byron. "She's precious to us."

"To me too," Byron said with a twinkle in his eye. "My precious," he whispered in my ear as we went down the stairs in a perfect imitation of Gollum from, Lord of the Rings.

Chapter Seven

At four we pulled up to Cindy's house. I hated to tell Cindy about another transgression of Jessie's. I got out of the car slowly. Byron helped me up Cindy's steps. Before we could knock the door was flung open by Cindy.

"How could you?" she asked. I took a step back almost falling off the porch. Byron caught me.

"How could I what?" I asked perplexed. Then it dawned on me. John told her.

"You're supposed to be my best friend!" She was so angry she balled up her fists and her knuckles were white.

"I am your best friend," I said.

"Then why didn't you tell me Jessie was pregnant?" she yelled. I cringed.

Byron still behind me said,"Let's take this inside." He pushed me through the door past Cindy. John and Joan sat in the living room. John sat straight in a chair, as stoic as usual.

Joan, an elementary school teacher sobbed as she sat on the sofa. Much to my surprise AJ sat in one of the other chairs.

"AJ? It's been like forever," I said. I limped over to him. He sat much like John did with his back ramrod straight. He wore an Air Force uniform with the standard military hair cut. His dark eyes stabbed at me. I always thought AJ was handsome with his thick head of black hair, his dark eyes and olive complexion. His features were hard though. I thought if I ever came up on him in an alley I'd run the other way. He was tall—over six feet—but tended to be more on the lean side. He didn't seem interested in shaking my hand so I sat in a chair next to him instead. Byron stood next to me. My own personal guard cop. What was going on here? Cindy sat down on the sofa next to Joan. Joan's eyes puffy from crying looked at her mother. She was the closest in age to John. When Cindy married Justin Lewis, Jessie's father, Joey was two, Joan was three and John was seven. I doubt Joan remembered AJ much until she was ten when he started coming around wanting visitation rights. She thought her dad was Justin so it devastated her. Joey was nine but went with the flow and John was fourteen. He welcomed visits with his dad but always came home quieter than usual. When AJ started moving around in the Air Force the visits became fewer and fewer. Finally, it was mostly phone calls, presents on birthdays and Christmas. I wonder if John resented his dad for not being there for him.

I looked at Cindy. She twisted a tissue in her hands.

"Tell me about Jessie," she said. "I want to hear it from you."

I took a deep breath."I don't know any more than what John has probably told you already. Jessie was eight weeks pregnant when she died."

"So, you think she jumped off the top of the building because she was pregnant?" AJ asked his dark eyes boring into me.

"I don't know. I'm going on the assumption she might've been pushed but I don't have any evidence to back it up beside a hunch."

Byron cleared his throat."I guess this is as good of a time as any to tell you I heard from the M.E. and she's ruling Jessie's death a homicide." I felt his fingers dig into my shoulder to keep me from jumping up. The room exploded, everyone talking at once, all trying to outdo the other. Cindy came over to Byron asking him to explain. He held up his hands. "Please, sit down, Cindy. I'll answer your questions if I can. One at a time." Cop speak for no effing way would I tell you a thing.

"What is the evidence?" John wanted to know.

Byron shook his head."Can't tell you except to say it's consistent with her being pushed off the building. The M. E. is still running tests."

"When will you know for sure?" Cindy asked.

"Don't know."

"So, this is now a real police investigation, not some half-hearted one led by a has-been cop?" AJ asked. He meant me. *Jerk.*

"Hey!" I said. He ignored me. He got up to shake Byron's hand.

"Thank goodness there's a real cop on the case now." I let it go. Everyone was under stress.

"Will there be a trial? I mean, will I have to testify?" Joan squeaked from the couch. She taught kindergarten, it was her first teaching job. She loved it and the kids seemed to love her. I softened toward her.

"No, Joanie, you won't have to testify," I said smiling at her. She glared back at me.

"Don't call me that. My name is Joan." *Yikes*. Resentment thy name is Joan. I cringed.

"Leave Mel alone, Joan," Cindy said. "She was only trying to help."

"Help what? If she was so much help why didn't she save Jessie? I mean she was the cop wasn't she? Isn't that what cops do? Save people? Where was she when Jessie was so messed up she'd come home in the middle of the night so high she couldn't find the bathroom? Or so high she'd throw up all night?" Joan was on a roll.

I felt Byron squeeze my shoulder again. "Yeah, where was Mel when Jessie was doing porn movies or being a stripper?" She turned bright eyes on me. "Where was Mel when her sweet Jessie was sleeping with every boy she could find in high school? Or when she began cutting herself with a razor blade when she was 13?" I gasped and so did Cindy. Neither one of us knew anything about that. Joan looked triumphant at me then at her mom. "She even slept with some of her male teachers in high school. She'd come home after sneaking out and tell me all about it. I never wanted to hear it but she told me anyway."

"Did you know who her current boyfriend was?" Byron asked.

Joan shook her head."No, after she moved out she stopped talking to me and if you want to know the truth, I was glad. I hated hearing all the sordid details of who did what to whom. She slept with anyone who looked cross-eyed at her. She started when she was in middle school. I took her to the free clinic in town to get her on birth control pills. We pretended she was sixteen. I let her use my ID." She took a breath. "After she got on the pills she really let loose. She'd sleep with total strangers she met on the street. Remember that shopping trip we took when I was eighteen in order to get my college clothes and Jessie was fifteen?" Joan was looking at Cindy who was very pale. She nodded slightly. "What a joke that was. Her goal was to sleep with someone at every store, customer, manager, it didn't matter. I was so embarrassed. She went into the dressing room with a guy and when she came out the knees of her jeans were all wet. I pointed to them and she said that there was water on the floor. I was so disgusted. I wanted to turn around and come home but she insisted we stay overnight. Once we checked into our hotel she took off. I didn't see her until the next morning when we were supposed to check out. I was going out of my mind with worry. But, did she care? No, all she cared about was herself, she was a selfish, selfish girl and I'm glad she's dead. It was only a matter of time. She deserved what she got," Joan now satisfied with her tirade smiled. Cindy got up went over to Joan and slapped her across the face making Joan's head whip to the side. Byron went over to Cindy to grab her hand before she could strike Joan again. Joan held her cheek with one hand, a horrified look on her face. She ran out of the room sobbing.

Cindy jerked her arm out of Byron's hand. "Anyone else care to comment on the nature of my daughter who is now lying dead in a coffin?" No one said a word. Cindy left the room. I went to follow her but Byron held me back.

"Let it rest for now, Mel. Let's go. Give Cindy a call later." It seemed like the best advice.

In the car I pondered a few things that seemed inconsistent to me.

"If Jessie started cutting in middle school and started sleeping with boys, it's a red flag for sexual abuse," I said.

"It can be a red flag," Byron pointed out. "It can also be a sign of undiagnosed Bipolar

Disorder or even a personality disorder. Did Jessie ever tell you about any abuse she was going through?"

"No, but there was her step-dad and two older brothers in the house. Any one of them could've been an abuser."

"Don't jump to conclusions, Mel. We have no evidence she was abused. I'll question the boys and AJ, see if anything shakes out."

"Better see if any sex offenders live in the neighborhood too," I said.

"Yes, Mel," Byron said.

"Oh and see if those bouncers at Barre really are gay. Maybe one of them is the father of Jessie's baby. I think that whoever got her pregnant is the one who killed her."

"I know you do, Mel. Let me do my job, okay? Jacobs and I will handle it from now on. You are officially off the case."

"Cindy hasn't fired me," I said with a smug smile.

"She will now that she knows I am investigating." *Damn it.*

I dropped Byron at his car before pulling into my garage. He promised he'd call me later. I itched to know what he would be finding out from Emma Holmes, the Medical Examiner. We used to joke about her last name calling her Sherlock, the nickname stuck so to her colleagues she was Sherlock. I went in the house and sat down. I dug out my iPhone and punched in the number for the M.E.'s office. It rang and rang. Finally, one of Sherlock's assistants picked it up.

"M.E.'s office, Karen speaking."

"Hi, Karen, this is Mel Thompson. Is Sherlock there?"

"Hi, Mel! How are you doing?"

"Better. I miss your spectacular coffee." Karen laughed a throaty laugh.

"I bet you do." Karen was notorious for using left over coffee grinds to make the swill they served in the M.E.'s office. "I'll see if the doctor is busy. Hang on."

A couple of minutes later I heard a click. "Mel! How the hell are you?" Why was everyone asking me that?

"I'm starting to rally again. Look, the reason I called is that Byron told me that the Jessie Lewis case is now a homicide."

"I heard that you and Williams were an item again, true or false?"

"True," I said.

"Ha! Just a minute. Hey, Karen, you owe me a sawbuck, Williams is back with Thompson." She laughed. "I'm back. Glad that you two hooked up again. Now you know that since you are no longer on the force I am forbidden to give you any information relating to an open murder case, right?"

"Right." I waited a beat.

"Let me take this in my office, Mel. Karen!" She shouted in my ear. "Hang this up when I tell you too."

"I'm here," she said a couple of minutes later. "Karen! Hang up the other phone." I heard an audible click. "That woman drives me up the proverbial wall," she said with a smile in her voice. "I have to tell her every move to make."

"Really? Every move?" I knew that she and Karen were a couple.

"Well, not every move," she laughed. "She comes up with some pretty creative ways to entertain me, let me tell you."

"Sherlock, about Jessie Lewis?"

"Right, right. If Williams or that loud-mouth partner of his finds out I said anything, they'll have my head."

"I won't breathe a word. I need to know what you found."

She clicked into professional mode. "Her injuries were consistent with being pushed off the ledge. There were defensive wounds on her arms and it appeared she scratched her attacker, there is skin underneath the nails."

"DNA sent?" I asked.

"What, do you think I'm a rookie, Thompson? Yes, DNA sent out. I asked them to put a rush on it. I did a tox screen and she had been ingesting large amounts of alprazolam, too much for one person. Probably made her dizzy and unsteady on her feet. Wouldn't take much to shove her over. My best guess is whoever fed her the alprazolam pushed her."

"Was it hers or did it belong to someone else?"

"Hers. The bottle fell with her. Her name was on the prescription bottle. She was taking it for anxiety, 0.5 milligrams once or twice a day."

"Who prescribed it?"

"Her family doc. I already called him. Said she came in about a month ago and asked for something for anxiety. He gave her a thirty day supply. No questions asked."

"But she had more than the 0.5 in her system when she died?" I asked. I stretched my leg out wishing I had my ice pack.

"Xanax or alprazolam is a short acting benzodiazepine, meaning it's out of your system pretty quickly. Whoever gave her more must've given it to her in the hours preceding her death."

"Okay, defensive wounds, drugs in her system, anything else?"

"You know she was pregnant?"

"I heard."

"What you didn't hear and this is for your ears only, not the family's ears. It looks as though someone tried to abort it but there were pieces left."

"Someone? You think Jessie tried to do it?"

"Not sure. It was done before she died though. My guess is she started cramping and maybe bleeding, might've thought she was miscarrying. Either she still had a ways to go and the cycle was interrupted by her death, or she might've had to go to a clinic to get a D&C to clean her out."

"Tell Byron about it, maybe he can canvas the clinics, see if anyone remembers her."

"Mel, honey. Stop telling me to do my job. I am perfectly capable of doing it without your help. Although I do miss you around here."

"I'm sorry, Sherlock, I get into this cop mode and I don't know how to shut it off."

"You are forgiven only if you agree to come to dinner. Friday at seven. Bring a date if you want. Anyone but that obnoxious cop you are currently sleeping with."

"I'm sorry to have to break it to you, Sherlock but we don't get much sleeping done."

"Yuck, heterosexual sex makes me sick to my stomach. Karen! Get in here and talk to Mel while I go throw up." I laughed.

"I'll see you at seven on Friday, Sherlock. Call me if anything new shows up with the Lewis case."

"Will do, Mel. Glad you are doing better." She hung up. I smiled. Not only was Sherlock an excellent M.E. but before she decided to be a doctor she went to the Culinary Institute in France and worked as a five star chef before deciding she'd rather be a M.E. I looked forward to her culinary creation.

Almost as soon as I hung up the phone, it rang again. I looked at the number before answering. ST. MATTHEW's the name read.

"Hello?"

"Ah, good, I caught you." *Father Mark.*

"Father Mark, it's good to hear from you. I thought the memorial went well." All except for the part afterwards at Cindy's.

"I want you to come to dinner next week. Any night except Wednesday, that's the night I do Bingo for the nursing home. Are you free on Tuesday around six?"

"Yes, thanks." Wow, two dinners out this week? I was popular.

"Great, see you then, Mel." He hung up. Smiling I got up, forgetting about my leg, like I usually do when I am not in pain and crashed unladylike to the floor. "DAMN IT ALL TO HELL!" I screamed. I banged my elbow on the coffee table on the way down and it tingled.

I hauled myself up by holding onto the table. I limped over to where I had stashed my cane. I used it to hobble into the kitchen to make some coffee. I sat in the kitchen waiting for it to brew. I took out my notebook and made new notes. I wasn't officially off the case yet and I wanted to know who killed Jessie as much as Cindy did.

It hurt Jessie hadn't come to me if she had been abused by one of her brothers or her step-father. He was the most likely candidate in my opinion. Cindy told me he used to get physical with her and that's why she left him. In my mind, one kind of abuse led to another. Did Cindy know about the sexual abuse but wasn't talking about it? I took my cup of coffee—now that it was done—out on the patio. I grabbed a sweater hanging on the back of a chair. I knew it would be chilly out there but I felt like I needed to clear my head. I sat sipping the coffee letting my thoughts wander. Something didn't feel right about this. Something that I was missing, but, what?

Chapter Eight

I spent the rest of the day in bed trying to stave off a migraine. You'd think with all the pain pills I took a migraine would be out of the question. *Nope.* Had one. The phone rang off and on. None of the calls were from Cindy so I let it go to voice mail. I didn't bother to listen to any of them though.

Sometime in the night when I woke up after my pain pills wore off I noticed the migraine had gone. After taking another pill, I decided if my head was still better in the morning, I'd go to church at St. Matt's.

Going to Mass had become somewhat of a ritual for me. It comforted me to go through all the same motions I had done as a child and teenager. I didn't know if I still believed in God but there was something familiar about going to Mass on Sunday mornings. On Saturdays I often went to confession. But I rarely had anything to confess about.

"Bless me father for I have sinned, it's been

one month since my last confession."

"Go ahead my child." Mark, Father Mark. I recognized his voice.

"I don't have much. I got impatient with myself again for not being able to do what I used to do. I failed to return a phone call from a friend. I yelled at my neighbors for being too loud at night when I wanted to sleep." I couldn't think of any others. The big ones, the ones where I confessed I missed my old life and being a cop I didn't speak of. I didn't mention my loss of faith either. It didn't seem worth mentioning.

"Two Hail Mary's, one rosary and stop yelling at your neighbors, Mel. Oh Father in your mercy please forgive this sinner."

"In the name of the Father, the Son and the Holy Ghost," I said as I crossed myself sliding the screen that separated us closed. The confessional was a small box-like compartment attached to another one. In between there were screens that closed and opened by sliding them. A hard wooden bench where you could sit took up most of the interior space of the compartment.

Some of the churches let parishioners confess face-to-face but I couldn't do that. I left the confessional just as Father Mark was leaving his. I wasn't supposed to know who he was and he wasn't supposed to know who I was either. We were anonymous so parishioners could "confess" their sins easier. Only I knew who was on the other side of the screen from me and he knew who I was. I smiled at him as he shut the confessional door behind him.

"Hello Mel," he said as if he hadn't just been talking to me.

"Hello yourself, Father Mark. How are you?"

"I'm fine. You?" His violet eyes searched mine. Most of the priests at St. Matt's were old wizened men who smelled bad and looked worse. Father Mark not only looked young and handsome, he smelled just like Old Spice. A memory I had of my father, brief though it was, touched me. I distinctly remember drinking in that smell of aftershave when I was with him.

"I'm okay." He searched my face then put

his hand on my arm.

"You don't look okay, want to talk about it? You could come to dinner, I was supposed to do a class for a couple about to be engaged but they broke up," he grinned. "Seven? Millie is cooking pot roast with carrots and potatoes."

"Instead of Tuesday or in addition to?" I asked, adding a grin.

"I'm sure Millie won't mind seeing you on Tuesday too." Millie was the elderly housekeeper sans cook of the rectory. She had been cooking and cleaning for the reigning priest since she was in her twenties. No one knew how old she was exactly but she remembered voting for Truman. Or so she said. She could still cook though. "I have a sudden yearning for pot roast," I said.

"See you at seven," Father Mark took his hand off my arm and walked to the altar genuflecting before picking up some objects there and putting them in the cupboard underneath.

At seven, on the dot—it wouldn't do to be late in Millie's eyes—I rang the bell. Millie, dressed in a black dress that reached just above her ankles opened the door. Her eyes lit up behind her black framed glasses. She wore her hair in a slick backed bun that stretched her face so far back she didn.t need a face lift. She placed gnarled fingers on my wrist.

"Come in Detective Thompson, Father Mark is expecting you for drinks in the parlor." Her voice was shaky but her grip was firm. She was a tiny woman who probably weighed less than ninety pounds. She walked with a steady gait to the parlor and announced me.

"Detective Thompson." She indicated with a gesture that I should go into the room.

"It's Ms. Thompson now, Millie. I'm not a cop anymore." She bowed her head as if this information was too much for her to bear. Father Mark had been sitting in a brown leather chair next to a fireplace. The room was dark, filled with floor to ceiling bookcases that contained the various books the priests had collected over the years. The shelves held everything from Cervantes. *Don Quixote* to the latest legal thriller by Tom Clancy. Father Mark stood up as I entered the room.

"Glad you could make it, Mel," he said, extending his hand. He took my hand in both of his, one over the other. He looked me in the eye as he clasped my hand in his large ones. "Have a seat, wine?"

"Can't, pain meds, but you go ahead."

"One of the few vices that priests are allowed to have is alcohol. I have a fully stocked bar, mostly for the bishop when he comes to call." He laughed as he poured me a glass of soda. He handed it to me.

I took a sip. "Thanks." I wandered over to one of the shelves looking over the titles of the books.

"See anything you want to borrow?" Father Mark asked.

"I'm fine." I turned back toward him. He gestured to the brown leather chair that faced the other one.

“Please, sit down.” He poked at the fire to get the flames to go higher before sitting down on the other chair. “Tell me how you are doing after your injury, Mel.”

“I seem to be coping. I miss being a cop but, I know I can’t go back to it. I don’t feel like I fit in anywhere anymore.” Unexpected tears sprang up. I blinked them away. Father Mark had on what I called his “priest face” the one that said – tell me more—if he asked me how I felt about it I swear I’d smack him one. I sighed.

“Go on,” he said.

I watched the flames dancing in the fireplace. “The pain is bad at times and when that happens I’m glad I don’t have a nine to five to go to. But, other times when the pain isn’t so bad, like now, I want to be back at work doing something, anything. I feel so useless.”

“You are still a young woman, Mel. Have you talked to anyone about this?”

I laughed. “Now you sound like Byron, no, I haven’t. And, before you ask, I’m not going to.”

"How are you and Byron holding up as a couple? I know he moved out when you first got shot." My word gets around fast.

I shrugged. "We're dealing."

He took another sip of his wine.

"I really think you should talk to someone, Mel. It's important to get closure on your life before and to be able to go on with your life now, not as it was, but, now, from this moment forward." He ran a hand through his thick golden blond hair. If he wasn't a priest I would've gone after him long before this. He turned turquoise blue eyes on me.

"Closure is a bunch of crap," I said. He laughed so hard he spit out his whiskey that he just sipped. I grinned. He mopped up the front of his cassock with a napkin. He turned his million dollar smile on me.

"You have a way with words, Mel. Ever think about becoming a writer?"

"Nope."

"Tell me more about closure," he said. I knew he was trying to get me to talk.

"All they ever tell people is that once a certain amount of time has gone by you'll be able to stop grieving for insert-word-here, your significant other, your sister, your best friend's daughter, your job…whatever. All it means is that they no longer want to hear about your grief. No one wants to hear that I'm still in pain 22 out of 24 hours or that I'm so scared I'll never be able to be a functioning human being again much less hold down a job. Or that Byron will get so fed up taking care of a gimp that he'll leave me."

I took a deep breath. Now it was my turn to be on a roll. "Or that I won't be able to go up the stairs to go to bed, or that I won't be able to get undressed or dressed by myself or a hundred other things. You think people want to hear about that crap? No. All they want you to do is shut up about it and move on." There, I said my piece. I took a sip of my Coke chomping on a piece of ice.

"I get it, Mel. I do. You feel ripped off and that life isn't fair and you are pissed about it."

"Damn right I am."

"And, you should be. It isn't fair that you, a good cop, was shot by some bad guys or that your best friend's daughter was murdered. It all sucks."

"I've never heard you talk this way before, Father," I said, staring at him with what I'm sure is a look of astonishment on my face.

"I'm tired too, Mel. Tired of the poor, the homeless, the hands always out for more. Save me, Father; tell me what to do, Father; hear my confession, Father." It was his turn to sigh.

"We should have our own pity party—oh wait, we are." I said.

Father Mark laughed. "Don't be too upset about Jessie, Mel. You'll see her again in heaven, I truly believe that."

"You had me until the whole heaven bit."

"You don't believe anymore? Is that why you stopped coming to church?"

"Why would God let me be shot? Why would God let Jessie be killed by someone?"

"It wasn't God, it was Satan acting through a human."

"Can't Satan do his own dirty work?"

"No, he has to have a human to work with, a vessel if you will."

I shook my head."It's all random, Father. All of it. I was in the wrong place at the wrong time. Jessie made someone mad at her who pushed her, maybe a little too hard and she went over. Maybe whoever did it didn't intend for her to die."

"We'll never know, will we?" he said.

Just at that moment Millie popped her head in."Dinner is served," she said. She wrinkled her nose at Father Mark as he walked by her.

"Oh, sorry, Millie, I spilled some whiskey on myself. Let me go change into a clean shirt."

Millie led me to the table showing me to a seat. I sat down playing with my water glass. In the center of the table was a sculpture of a small dog. I lifted it up inspecting it. The detail was intricate. I smiled putting it back down when Father Mark came back into the room.

"One of yours?" I indicated the sculpture.

"Yes."

"It's lovely."

Father Mark nodded. "Thanks for noticing." In his spare time Father Mark did woodworking. He made furniture too. His pieces were full of finely carved details.

A young boy, probably one of the altar boys, had been commissioned to help serve us.

He looked nervous but he served us clear French Onion soup without spilling any. I smiled at him. He looked to be about twelve.

Father Mark saw me staring at the boy. "That's Cory, he lives down the street. He's doing penance for soaping the rectory's windows last week."

"Hi Cory, thanks for the soup." Cory blushed but didn't say anything. He bowed before heading back to the kitchen. The soup was delicious. We talked in between spoonfuls. A good hearty French bread was also served with thick butter lathered on each slice.

"Hasn't Millie ever heard of high cholesterol?"I stage whispered to Father Mark. He shook his head at me but his eyes were twinkling. The pot roast was juicy, the carrots crisp and the potatoes were served with gravy so good I could feel my arteries hardening as I lapped up the few drips I had left on my plate with a piece of bread. "Yum," I declared. Millie and Cory cleared the plates and brought in two slices of Apple Pie topped with scoops of vanilla ice cream. On the side of the plate was a slice of cheddar cheese. "Oh, what the heck," I said digging into the pie. Father Mark did the same. Millie brought in coffee and brandy once the pie was eaten.

"Care to have coffee in the parlor or stay here?" Father Mark asked, standing up.

"The parlor is fine, I like the fireplace." I carried my coffee sans brandy to the parlor. This time I sat in the chair that Father Mark had been sitting in. He took the other one. He added a big splash of brandy to his coffee along with a huge dollop of whipped cream on top.

"Reminds me of Irish Whiskey," he said taking a sip. I laughed because he now had a whipped cream moustache. He wiped it off with a grin. "You're not having any brandy?"

"I have to drive home and anyway, I can't. Pain meds, remember?"

"I am not driving anywhere," he said his words slightly slurred. *Uh oh.* Maybe it was time for me to go. Father Mark looked at me. "I wanted to tell you, Mel. Before I told the bishop. I'm leaving Beechton."

"Oh? Why? Are you being transferred?" I knew that the Catholic Church did that sometimes.

"Yes, to Ireland. It's my choice."

"I'll miss you," I said, taking a sip of my coffee. He nodded.

"I'd like to see you before I go if that's all right with you. Let's do dinner Sunday night after the evening mass instead of Tuesday. It'll be my last night here. The following Monday I'm flying to Dublin."

"Yes, I'd like that." I stood up looking for my cane then I remembered I left it in the car. "I'll see myself out, Father Mark. Thank Millie for me. That dinner was great." His eyes clouded over for an instant then cleared. Puzzled, I stared at him. The corners of his mouth drew up but it wasn't any kind of a smile. I wiggled my fingers at him as I made my way to the door.

Chapter Nine

I woke up to frost. I had an appointment with my spine doc. I hoped he'd tell me I could get rid of the cane once and for all. I took my usual morning pain pills, had coffee, got dressed. By the time I got to the doctor's office the pain meds had kicked in.

"Hey, Mel, how's the pain today?" My doctor was a dead ringer for Doogie Howser except I knew for a fact he was older than he looked because I asked him at my first appointment.

"It's okay."

"Give me a number."

"5 out of ten once the pain pills are on board."

"And before that?"

"10 out of 10." He was manipulating my leg as I talked. He gave me directions to follow. Walk, sit, stand. I felt like a Golden Retriever. He pressed on my back, told me to lie down on the exam table.

"Describe the pain to me."

"Same pain, burning tingling hot poker down my leg and toothache in back."

He nodded. "All of the time or some of the time?"

"Depends. On what? I have no idea."

"It's been almost a year since your injury, is that right?"

"Right."

"Let's schedule another x-ray, make sure that bullet hasn't moved. I'm still reluctant to do surgery given the proximity of the bullet to the spine."

"Do I still need the cane?" I asked eyeing the cane.

"Yep, 'fraid so. That leg is still very weak. Don't want you take a tumble." Yeah. I didn't mention the two falls I had recently. He made a note on his computer that sat in the corner of the exam room. "Any recent falls?" It was as if he read my mind.

"A couple. Fell off the couch, lost my

balance on a floor," I said. Yeah, after two goons kicked the cane out from under me.

"Be careful, we don't want that disc to bulge out anymore than it is, do we?" Who's this "we" doctors are always talking about? He consulted his computer again. "Let's keep the meds the same except increase the one at bedtime, maybe it'll help with the morning pain." He looked up at me. "Any questions?"

"Nope."

"Then I'll see you in a month or sooner if your pain gets worse. I'll have the front desk call you when your x-ray is scheduled. No hurry on that." He shook my hand then left. I limped over to the cane. What if I accidentally on purpose left it here in the corner? They'd probably call me up and tell me to come get it. I grabbed it and headed out to the checkout desk.

The phone rang as I got in the car. *Byron.* "Hello?"

"How'd the doctor go?"

"Fine. Increased one of my pain pills at bed. That's it. Oh, and another x-ray. Keep using my cane. Don't fall. Blah, blah, blah."

"Well, good." The phone call felt awkward. "How'd you dinner with Father Mark go?"

"Good. I ate too much. He's moving to Ireland to take over a parish there in a couple of weeks."

"Too bad, he's very charismatic." This from the guy who hasn't been to church since he was a teenager. I sat staring out at the cars pulling in and out of the doctor's driveway.

"Want some good news for a change?"

"Sure."

"Jacobs has decided he doesn't hate you and that you are good for me."

I laughed. "Oh? How come?"

"I brought in bagels for the crew this morning and coffee. I haven't done that in ages."

"That's nice." Something was bothering me but it wouldn't come to the surface. "Did you check out the alibi's for Barre and company? And any former abuse charges on AJ? Have you talked to Jessie's friends about who the possible boyfriend might be?"

"Mel," he said in that exasperated you-know-I-can't-tell-you-anything voice.

"Never mind. Look, I can't drive and talk at the same time so I better go."

"Since when?"

"Before I forget, we're invited to Karen's and Sherlock's house for dinner Friday night."

"She told me. Want me to pick you up?"

"No, I'll drive myself. See you on Friday." I hung up. The phone rang again. I glanced at the screen.

"Cindy, hello," I said, surprised. I hadn't heard from her at all since the fiasco at her house on Saturday.

"I have a favor to ask." No hello first?

"Okay."

"Can you go with me to Jessie's apartment to help me box up her things? The landlady called and her rent is up. She wants to rent it out again." I assumed the cops were done with it.

"Sure, what time?"

"Is now a good time?" Cindy asked.

"I'll be right there." I took a deep breath. On

the one hand I was happy that Cindy wanted me to help her but on the other hand I didn't know if this would be too emotional for both of us. That Hello Kitty bag was already making me tear up. I needed to get a grip. I had to be strong for Cindy's sake. I figured if I acted stoic, she might too. At least that was my hope.

Cindy waited in her car until I had parked. The two of walked (well, I limped) to the entrance. Cindy had a key. She opened the door and we went in. The last time I had been at Jessie's, before I got shot, the place was a mess. Then, when Byron and I were here, it was neat and clean. Now, it looked as though a tornado had gone through it. No, two tornadoes. Books were torn from the shelves; magazines lay scattered on the floor along with letters, scraps of paper, pieces of the couch cushions lay on the floor. Cindy started to take a step inside but I blocked her with my arm.

"No, you can't contaminate the scene. Stay put while I call Byron." She stood in place her eyes wide with questions. He answered right away. “Byron? I don’t think your guys did this but Jessie’s apartment is trashed. Cindy and I are there now. We were going to box up Jessie’s things. I hope the cops didn’t do this.”

“No, I did a cursory search but, saw no reason to ask the crime tech team to come in. She was pushed off the building, not murdered in her apartment. You sure it was tossed?” Cop speak for trashed. I didn’t answer. Byron cleared his throat. “Of course you’re sure, I’m sorry, Mel. I’ll send the crime techs over there right now. Wait outside for them.” As if he had to tell me. I nodded at Cindy after I hung up.

“Byron wants us to wait outside,” I said. “Someone was looking for something, no telling what. Come on.” I led her outside. We stood on the concrete slab that doubled as a porch waiting. I idly leaned on my cane for support. I needed to sit down. “I’m heading to the car, I need to sit,” I said. I put my cane down but it slipped and landed in the bushes. I nearly fell but grabbed the window box perched outside the window. Part of it came off and it now hung at a crazy angle.

"Oops," I said trying to straighten it. Something shiny caught my eye. I had dislodged some dirt when I hung onto the window box. I reached into it and pulled out a wooden crucifix with a carved Jesus on it hung from a silver chain.

"Oh, that's Jessie's. Was Jessie's. Father Mark gave it to her when she was thirteen. He carved it himself." I brushed the dirt off it and held it up. Other than it needed a good wiping off, it looked okay.

"How did it get in the window box?" I mused.

Cindy shrugged. "Jessie always wore it, said it was her good luck charm. Maybe she bent over to plant something and the chain broke." I inspected the chain for damage. None.

"The chain isn't broken," I said.

"Well, maybe it's another chain, I don't know," she said. She held out her hand for it.

"Is it all right if I keep it, Cindy? As a reminder of Jessie. Please?" I held it by the chain, I knew that fingerprints would not be possible to get off so small an object but I wanted to keep it anyway. She shrugged again.

"Fine." Both her hands went into her coat pockets. She wore a denim jacket over jeans with black and white tennies on. She tapped one of her tennies. "Where are those cops? It's cold out here."

"Winter is on its way," I said. I mentally hit myself in the forehead. What kind of a stupid statement is that? "Look, Cindy I…" But, any comment I was about to make was cut short by the arrival of a black van filled with Crime Scene techs. Four of them. They shooed us away stringing yellow crime scene tape around. I kept my mouth shut about the crucifix and hoped Cindy would do the same. She seemed uninterested in me. She peered in the window several times. Finally, one of the techs came out. A woman on the way to the van. I stopped her with a hand on her arm. She wasn't anyone I knew. To her I was just another civilian.

"Are you going to be much longer? We need to box up her things."

"An hour or so."

“Looks like someone did toss it,” I said watching her eyes for confirmation. She nodded ever so slightly.

“Maybe. Come back in an hour, we’ll be done by then.” I relayed the message to Cindy. She nodded. Her gaze was everywhere but at me.

“Let’s do this another day, tomorrow at 11?”

I nodded. “Fine, see you then,” I said as she walked away toward her car.

Every fiber in my being screamed out to her to come back and talk to me but I let her go. Maybe she’d come around in time. But, then again, maybe she wouldn’t.

I should’ve given the crucifix to the Crime Scene techs. Fingerprints are difficult to pull off wood and I wanted something of Jessie’s.

* * *

I was getting ready to go when my phone rang. *Cindy.* I picked it up. “On my way, running a bit late this morning, maybe a Starbucks run is in order,” I said.

“Don’t bother showing up,” she said in a too-calm voice.

"Oh? Why not?" I sat down on the edge of the bed.

"The police were here yesterday. Questioning John about Jessie. They also questioned AJ about his involvement with his step-daughter." I didn't say anything. What was there to say? "I know it was you that put the police up to this. How could you accuse John and Joey of such a thing? They loved Jessie like she was their own sister."

"I thought Joey was in San Francisco," I said.

"He is. He called me last night to tell me the San Francisco police had been to his house to question him as a favor to the Beechton police. He was mortified. So was his roommate, Jeff."

"Isn't Jeff his partner?" I asked. I know it was snarky but I was pissed at her too. She had no right to be mad at me. I know that grief does horrible things to people but ruining our friendship?

"What do you mean, 'partner'?" she asked. "Are you insinuating Joey is gay? He went to prom with a girl, remember?" I took a deep breath. I did not want to have this conversation on the phone.

"Cindy, why do think Joey never comes home? John is so homophobic he threatened to beat Joey up once if he didn't stop being gay."

"Who told you that?"

"Joey. He loves you guys to pieces but he wants to be accepted for who he is, not who he sleeps with." Silence on the other end made me think she had hung up. "He hated that you didn't believe him last Christmas when he told you he was gay."

"I can't deal with this right now. I have to think about Jessie. I still can't believe you think anyone in our family had anything to do with abusing Jessie. If she was being abused why wouldn't she tell me? I would've understood." Right. Like you understood about your son being gay?

"Maybe it was someone she thought she couldn't tell on," I countered.

"Oh, you mean like her step-brother or her

step-father?" she sneered.

"Or a neighbor, or teacher or family friend," I said. *Jeez!*

Cindy started sobbing. "I tried to do what was best for her. She was such a happy baby, always cooing and smiling. I remember her toddling toward me when she first learned how to walk, she was so adorable," she sobbed some more. I let her cry it out. "I don't know what happened. When she changed. One day she was this nice, happy little girl and the next she was this selfish, talking back kid who would sneak cigarettes out of her dad's jacket pocket and money out of my purse. Did I know she was sneaking out at night when she was fifteen? Yes, I did. I thought she was going through a phase that she'd get over it. I knew she was having sex but I didn't want to know with whom. I found the package of birth control pills so at least she was covered that way. I ignored it. I couldn't deal with it then, and I can't deal with it now."

"So, you have no idea when she began to change? Her grades in school were good in elementary school I recall."

"It wasn't until she was in middle school, but all kids have a rough time in middle school."

"Did you know about the cutting?"

"No, that I didn't know about. I wonder what happened to her? I don't suppose we'll ever know."

"Not unless someone tells us," I said beginning to warm up to the idea that Cindy had forgiven me.

"Someone like who?" she asked. "John? Joey? AJ? Maybe you think it was her own father who molested her? Is that what you think? Well, you can't ask him, HE'S DEAD!" She banged the phone down in my ear so hard I jumped. She must've smacked it down on a table. I rubbed my ear. She knew something hinky was going on with Jessie but she was too afraid to figure it out. Maybe it was Justin. If so, there would be no way we'd ever find out. But, if her father had been molesting her, then who killed her? It's kinda hard to rise up from the dead to kill someone unless you're a zombie and

I was pretty sure Justin wasn't a zombie. My money was on the step-father, AJ or John. Or someone she adored. Like her father. I sighed. *Please, don't let it be, Justin.* I liked him, he was good to Cindy and the kids and he adored me. Always a plus in my book. So different from AJ. Justin was a gentle poetic soul who loved Cindy and all the kids and they knew it. *No, it wasn't Justin who molested Jessie.*

I called Joey in San Francisco. He owned and operated his own art gallery in the Castro district, otherwise known as the "gay village" at the intersection of Market and 17th Streets. He answered on the first ring.

"Art for Art's Sake, this is Joey, how may I help you?"

"Hey, Joey, it's Mel Thompson."

"Mel? Mel, oh my God, how are you? Mom said you might call." I bet she did.

"Look, I'm sorry about sending the cops your way. Your mom said you were upset."

"Naw, just amused that you might think I molested my female step-sister. Honey, I've been gay since I was born and noticed the cute male doc who delivered me," he laughed then his tone turned serious. "So, do you think she was molested by someone? I mean, sexually? Is that why she was killed?"

"No, that's not why she was killed, Joey. I do think she was sexually abused by someone but, at this point I'm not sure we'll find out who did it."

"Was it, I mean, could it have been, dad? Or John?"

"I hope not."

"Yeah, me too."

"Do you remember when Jessie first started acting different? I mean you might not have noticed since you were only two years apart in age."

"I don't. Two years can make a big difference when you are kids. She had her friends, I had mine. It wasn't until I was a senior in high school that I came out to her."

"Oh?" I hadn't heard this.

"Look, Mel, I have a customer. Give me a

number and I'll call you back tonight around eight my time."

"Okay, thanks, Joey, nice to hear your voice."

"Yeah, me too." He hung up without saying goodbye. I didn't know if he'd call me back or not. I hit my forehead with my palm for real this time. I forgot all about the dinner with Karen and Sherlock! I'd be at their house. Well, maybe I could excuse myself around that time. I know that Byron would have a fit and fall in it—as my mother used to say—if he knew I was still investigating. What he didn't know wouldn't hurt him now, would it?

* * *

I went from a calorie-laden dinner filled with butter on Sunday courtesy of Millie to a culinary dream dinner on Friday. Sherlock outdid herself with pesto pasta, Italian bread drizzled with olive oil, salad with olives, oranges, pecans and peas and for dessert we had double-chocolate chunk brownies with real vanilla ice cream on top.

"So, how goes it with you, Mel?" Karen asked. We were in the after dinner coffee phase. The four of us sat in their living room. They had the whole my-furniture-looks-shabby-but-it-cost-more-than-your-years-salary look down. I bet the coffee table cost a mint. I was reluctant to put my leg up even though I wanted to. I shifted on the couch.

"I'm doing okay, I guess. How's life in the morgue?"

"Quiet," Karen said. "Except for when Sherlock is there, then all hell breaks loose."

"It does not," Sherlock said, glaring at Karen. I longed to ask Sherlock what she had found out so far about Jessie. I looked at Byron who shook his head slightly. *Fine.* No cop talk tonight.

"Tell me about your vacation," I said instead. I knew that Karen would drag out her laptop to show us pictures upon pictures of their Greece and Italy vacation. Byron moaned next to me. "Shush," I said as Karen went to get her laptop. Sherlock went in the kitchen to get more coffee.

"We'll be here for hours," Byron whispered.

"Pretend you like the pictures," I hissed back at him. He nodded again.

"Here we go," Karen said, setting up the laptop so that the pictures could be seen on their TV. "Now, this is the Parthenon, see Sherlock waving, she's that tiny speck way up high."

We were finishing up with the pictures when my phone buzzed in my pocket. I had put it on vibration. I startled when it began buzzing.

"You okay?" Byron asked. I got up and limped over to get my cane.

"Fine, just need to use the ladies, be back soon." I hightailed it down the hallway. Opened the door furthest from the kitchen, a guest bedroom and sat down on the bed before answering my phone.

"Hi, Joey, glad you called me back."

"Thanks, Mel. I can't talk long, Jeff is waiting dinner for me. Now, where was I?"

"You told Jessie you were gay when you were a senior and she was a sophomore."

"Right, she said she knew already. I laughed. Here I was worrying about it and she said she had known for years. Said she was cool with it. Said she had slept with girls too but she preferred boys."

"Did she say anything else?"

"Not really. Told me not to tell John or my step-father, was afraid they'd freak out. And, of course I didn't tell them until last Christmas and she was right, they freaked out. Even mom. Told me I was going through a phase. A phase. What a joke that was. Anyway, when I was a senior I had been accepted at Berkeley. I wanted Jessie to come with me but she refused. Said her life was there in Beechton. She said she needed to figure some things out. I wish I brought her with me." He sounded sad.

"So, you hadn't seen her since last Christmas?"

"No, we talked on the phone now and again but, that was all. I didn't know about the porn or the drugs until Mom told me. Jessie never mentioned either of those to me. I did know she was stripping though. That she told me." He paused.

"John said she called you right before she died. He said she wanted to come out to San Francisco to live with you and you refused to let her," I said.

"Look, Mel, since it's you I can say this. I loved Jessie; she was the sweetest thing when she was a little girl. But, I didn't trust her. I figured she'd either steal me blind, I mean I have some expensive art pieces here at the apartment, or she'd try to sleep with Jeff or both. I loved her but there is no way I wanted to live with her even for a short while." He paused again. "And, before you ask, yes, I feel guilty about that. If I had said yes, would she still be alive?"

"You had to do what was right for you and Jeff." Now it was my turn to hesitate. "Did your mom tell you that Jessie was pregnant when she died?"

"Yeah, you think the guy that did this to her killed her?"

"I do, yes. Any idea who she was sleeping

with?"

"The entire city of Beechton and surrounding areas," he said, not laughing. "I'm sorry but my sister would sleep with anything in pants or in skirts. She wasn't picky."

"I heard. Look, thanks again for calling me back, Joey. Sorry you couldn't make it for the memorial, Father Mark did a nice job."

"I have to go, Mel. Jeff is waiting." He hung up as usual without saying goodbye. I jumped when the bedroom door opened and Byron stuck his head in.

"Funny looking bathroom," he said. "You okay? Your leg bothering you?"

"No, I just needed to stretch out for a bit." I eyed the phone lying beside my leg hoping he wouldn't notice it. He sat down on the bed next to me.

He gave me a funny look. "Karen wants to know if you would like to stay to see a movie with them. I believe the choices are something with aliens, something without aliens, something with a kid who has an alien and something with a kid who has no alien but wants one."

I laughed. "Naw, I'm bushed. I'm going to bail, but you stay if you want."

He glanced at me. "I don't want. I want to go home with you." He nuzzled my neck and I swooned a little. Sherlock opened the door wide. She yelled down the hall.

"Hey, Karen, guess who is making out in the guest room?"

Chapter Ten

The papers were full of it. Another murder. This one more obvious. Patty Wilcox, the stripper who worked with Jessie. There had to be a connection between the two of them other than their work connection. I speed dialed Byron. He picked up.

“You heard?” he asked.

“I read it over my morning coffee, wonder what’s going to happen to her kid now?”

“Her sister was already taking care of him, I imagine she’ll continue,” he said.

“So, there’s a connection between Patty, Jessie and Barre, I’m thinking,” I said. No answer. “Byron?”

“I heard you, Mel. You know I can’t comment on a connection, if any.” He paused. “Before you say anything else please promise me you won’t go back to Barre.”

“I think you asked me that already,” I said

taking a sip of my coffee.

“And you never gave me a straight answer,” he said.

“I know you think that protecting me is your job, Byron, but, it isn’t. It’s my job to protect me. Barre had me shot because I made Jessie quit the biz. What if he had Patty shot because we talked to her about Jessie?”

“He’s an asshole, Mel, we all know that, but, show me the evidence that he had you shot, pushed Jessie off that building and had Patty shot and I’ll jump in there with you. Right now we don’t have squat.” I could tell he was rubbing the top of his head because he did that when he was frustrated.

“Are you going to talk to Patty’s sister again? What about ballistics, is there a bullet from Patty?”

“Mel, I’m only going to say this one more time, stay out of this case, don’t talk to any more witnesses and don’t impede my investigation. I mean it.” I didn’t know if I should salute the phone or hang up on him. I hung up. I downed another pain pill and dialed Cindy's number.

"Don't hang up, Cindy, please. I have to talk to you. Have you seen the newspaper this morning?"

"I glanced at it, why?"

"One of the strippers who worked with Jessie at Barre was murdered last night. Shot in front of the club." She gave a sharp intake of breath.

"You think there's a connection?"

"I do. Up for a road trip?"

"To Barre?"

"Yes and ask AJ if you can borrow one of his handguns. I don't have a weapon anymore."

"A gun? I'm not sure I should go if you are planning on shooting someone."

"I'm not planning on it, I just want it in case. Meet me out front in twenty and don't forget the gun."

"Roger," she said before hanging up. I hated to involve a citizen but I figured Barre wouldn't shoot both of us.

Instead of Cindy waiting outside her house, it was AJ. Cindy was nowhere in sight. He got in. He wore his battle fatigues along with a black tee shirt. His dark glasses mirrored my image back to me. I grinned at him.

"Hey, AJ. Where's Cindy?"

"She decided you needed me instead." Which means, he decided.

"Look, AJ, about the whole abuse issue I wanted to say…" But, before I could go on he held up a hand.

"You're just covering all the bases, like you were supposed to. No harm done."

"Did you bring me a gun for me?" I asked.

He shook his head. "No, you aren't licensed but I am." He pulled out a Glock from his pants pocket.

"You still in the military?" I thought he got out.

"Nope. Been out for a couple of months now."

"Then where'd you get the…never mind." I wasn't a cop any longer, I didn't need to know.

"Just don't use that thing unless we are up against a wall and someone is aiming to shoot at us, okay?"

"Okay," he said, licking his lips. I shivered not sure I could trust him. I had to admit that he was intimidating though with his broad shoulders, muscled upper arms and his I-don't-take-nothing-from-nobody attitude. Plus he was big. As big as Alejandro and Sven. I figured he could engage with them if he had to. Better him than me.

"Don't use it unless we're threatened," I said. I wanted to make sure he was listening.

"You don't have to tell me how to act around scumbags," he said, shoving the gun back in his pants pocket. Did he have other weapons too? All I had in my arsenal was my cane and a small spray can of air freshener. I reached across AJ to open the glove box.

"Excuse me," I said, pulling out the air freshener.

"What'cha gonna do with that?" he asked. "Freshen 'em up?" He guffawed at his own joke.

I smiled inwardly seething. I tried listening to my gut as I put the car in gear but my gut wasn't speaking to me right now.

Barre had the closed sign up. I banged on the door as hard as I could.

"What?" Alejandro opened the door, took one look at AJ and tried slamming the door shut. But, not fast enough. AJ had his steel-reinforced military combat boot in the doorway so the door couldn't close. AJ hadn't said a word so far. Alejandro looked at AJ, then at me. He shrugged. "Your funeral," he muttered opening the door to let us in.

I gestured he should lead the way to Barre's office. Unlike before, the mood in Barre was quiet, subdued. A pall hung over the club's atmosphere. I saw several girls huddled together, some of them were crying. I teared up briefly as I thought of Patty.

"Is the club closed because of Patty?" I asked as we followed Alejandro.

"Naw, boss just wanted the girls to have a day to themselves, he's nice that way. Caring."

Uh-huh. Alejandro knocked on the door. "Boss? Some people to see you, that nosy cop from before."

"Which cop from before?" he asked.

"Me," I said opening the door wider. AJ and I scooted in. AJ stood next to me as if he was my bodyguard, maybe he was. Alejandro did the same with Barre.

"Relax, boys. Alejandro make these nice people a drink. We're closed to honor Patty's memory today but, the bar is still open." I heard music start up. I turned questioning eyes to Barre. He waved a hand at the door. "Oh, we are only opening for special customers, Patty's friends and her regulars." The rich ones no doubt.

"Nothing for me," I said. AJ shook his head too. Alejandro went out, shutting the door.

"So, who's this strapping fellow? New beau?" Barre asked me.

"Friend of the family," I said. "Former military cop."

"Ah, well he looks it." He stared at AJ then

back at me. "What do you want Ms. Thompson. I thought we agreed you wouldn't come around here anymore."

"Let's see, what do I want?" I ticked off the list on my fingers. "I want to go back a year ago and not get shot by one of your goons," I said. He started to speak but before he could I went on. "Two," I ticked off another finger, "I want whoever shot me to rot in Hell, three, I want the killer of Jessie brought to justice and four, I want Patty's killer to be brought to justice." I stared at him. "Of course, all I need to do is prove it was you and presto. Jail time for you."

"Now, why would I shoot you, Ms. Thompson? And why kill off two of my best girls? Jessie was young and hot, she was already gaining a following among the connoisseurs of my film enterprise, Barre Media. And, Patty was one of my best dancers. Why would I kill the golden goose? Now I'm out two girls with no replacements in sight." He looked me up and down. "Except for that gimp leg of yours, you're still quite a looker, Thompson. Maybe we could make an exception in your case, have you strip with a cane, we could adorn it with ribbons." He snapped his fingers. "I know, get you one of those fancy ones with a top hat, have you wear a tux with tails only no top of course." He eyed me as if it would be a possibility. "Why don't you stand up and let me look at your assets a bit closer, hmm?" He stood up behind the desk and AJ took a step forward too. Barre sat back down. "No? Well, think about it. We can always use more help around the holiday season and Thanksgiving is right around the corner. If you have nothing else, I'm a busy man trying to run a business." He dismissed us with another wave of his hand.

"I'm not one of your employees, Barre," I said. "So waving your hand does nothing for me." I took a breath. "I know you had something to do with these killings and for the record, when I find out you did, I'm coming for you. I'm no longer a cop so I don't care that I'm not supposed to shoot the bad guys." I sat on the edge of my seat. "AJ? Show him my gun." AJ took out the Glock, it looked much bigger in this small room. AJ twirled it around his finger and put it back in his pocket. Barre blanched. “My pal here holds it for me and sometimes he uses it on bad guys and ya know what, Barre? He bought it off a street vendor so the serial numbers have been filed off. No tracing it back to me. Get my drift?” He nodded once.

I got up shoving my chair so hard it tumbled to the floor. I grabbed my cane and hit it across Barre’s desk making the papers fly off in all directions. He jumped back spilling the drink that had been sitting there all over the rest of the papers and him.

“Damn it, Thompson, look what you’ve done!” he bellowed. Alejandro rushed in. I pointed to the desk.

“Looks like your boss had a bit of an accident,” I said. “Come on, AJ, we’re done here.”

“Bitch,” Barre said as we left. I hesitated for a brief second, smiled and kept going.

Once we were in the car my hands gave way to shaking. AJ looked at me. He took off his mirrored sunglasses.

“Do you think that was wise? He’s going to be royally pissed at you now.”

“That’s the point. When he’s riled he’s going to make a mistake and when he does, I’ll nail him.”

“You’re no longer a cop,” AJ said. “You can’t arrest him.”

“I wasn’t talking about arresting him,” I said.

* * *

I needed to get into Barre to see the files. The only way to do that was to go in after the club closed. I drove to a city lot open all night for the third shift employees at the hospital nearby. I took two pain pills to compensate for the ensuing pain sure to follow a three block hike to Barre. I waited in the alley behind the club next to the dumpster. This was the kind of stuff Byron and I did on stakeouts except I was able to crouch down then and I didn’t have a cane. I hunkered down as low as I could so that anyone opening the back entrance wouldn't see me. I had on my standard nighttime stakeout gear, black pants, black tennies, black tee shirt with a hoodie. I had the hood pulled up over my hair. Voices came and went. I stiffened up and had to take a short breather while I walked out stiff muscles. I hoped no one had seen me. I stood next to the dumpster again. More voices. And sounds I recognized. *Yeew.* Two someones were getting it on on the other side of the dumpster. I heard, "give it to me baby" and "that's right, harder, harder." Wait, I recognized that voice. I straightened up only to see Byron grinning at me from the other side of the dumpster.

"Very funny," I said. He walked over to me. "How'd you know I was here?" I held up a hand. "Wait, a little birdie named AJ told you?" For an answer he whistled. "Yeah, nice."

"What did you think you could do in this situation? Beat them to death with your cane?"he asked, frowning at me.

"Maybe. I wanted to get inside and check

out Barre's files. There has to be a connection." He gave me an elbow.

"Well, come on then. Let's go see those files." I assumed he had a warrant. We went in through the front door, this time one of the women let us in. Jacobs waited for us just inside.

"Nice to see you again, Thompson," he said showing me his teeth.

"Likewise," I said. The three of us went straight to Barre's office. The girl went back to whatever it was she had been doing. There was no sign of Barre. "So, he was okay with this? You don't think he hid files?"

"Oh, I'm sure he did," Byron said. "We just have to find the right ones."

"You'd think in this day and age he'd have his files on his computer," I said. The three of us looked at each other simultaneously.

"We are idiots of the first degree," Byron said, sitting down at Barre's desk. "No wonder he didn't care if we had a warrant. All the important files are on his computer, probably at home."

"Another warrant?" Jacobs asked.

"Naw, no judge is going to give us two warrants unless we find something first." He got up. "Let's finish looking then call it a night. Hey, where you going, Mel?"

"I'm going to go talk to the girl that let us in, maybe she knows something."

"Keep us posted," Jacobs said pulling out a file drawer stuffed with papers. He moaned.

The woman was the only one sitting at the bar. I went up to her taking the stool next to her. It was no mean feat with my leg and my cane, let me tell you. She paid no attention to me.

"Hi, I'm Mel Thompson, I spoke to Patty before. I'm a Private Investigator." She didn't take her eyes from her drink. She was hunched over it like it was a bonfire and she was trying to eke out any warmth from it.

"I know who you are," she said with a husky too-many-cigarettes-smoked-and-too-much-whiskey-drank type voice. Now she turned to look at me. Her hollowed out cheekbones and sunken eyes gave me a clue as to where she got her calories from. Not to mention her waif-like arms thin beyond starvation standards.

"Jesus," I said, before I thought. Then, "Sorry."

"Don't be, it's no secret. I'm dying. AIDS related complex or something like that. Was HIV positive for years. Finally caught up to me."

"Don't most take meds to keep it at bay for years?" I asked.

"I never had the money for pills," she said.

"And Barre knows?"

"Yeah. I got it from a customer back in the day before us girls were tested much. He let me stay on to help him out. I do mostly office work, hire the girls and the bouncers, keep tabs on the dancers. All the boring stuff he doesn't want to do." She looked back at her drink. "I'm Ruby. Used to have this gorgeous red hair that fell down to my butt. Guys couldn't keep their hands off it, ya know? It all fell out. I'm bald as a peacock. Wear this wig so as to not freak out anyone."

"The wig isn't red," I said. It was black, and

short.

"Didn't want it to remind me of what I used to have," she said. "Why are you here?"

"First, I'm shot in the alley, then my friend's daughter is pushed off a building and then Patty is shot. It seems like too big a coincidence. I'm just looking for the truth." She guffawed at that. She began coughing then took a drink.

"You okay?" I asked.

She nodded. "Barre had nothing to do with you getting shot. Or with Jessie's death." The part she left out interested me.

"But, he did have something to do with Patty's death?"

She shrugged. "I'm not about to turn on the only person who didn't give up on me," she said. Fair enough.

"What happened with Patty?" I asked.

"Got too mouthy with the customers, always wanting more than her share. One of her regulars is someone who doesn't want his name thrown about town. She threatened to expose him if he didn't set her and her boy up in a small house, give her an allowance, clothes, the whole bit. He refused, said that no two-bit hooker would take him for all he was worth. She shot at him, he shot back. Patty's dead and he's still walking around. Don't ask me for his name, won't give it."

"Truth?" I asked.

"Truth," she said. "Barre had nothing to do with it. Get me?" I nodded. Well, he sort of did but indirectly.

"You know who Jessie's boyfriend was?" I asked. "Patty said he came in on Thursdays."

"He always came in through the back and waited in one of the lap dancing private rooms. Paid in cash only. Showed up at midnight every Thursday. Never got a good look at him but she was scared of him."

"Oh?"

"She was afraid he'd kill her if he found out about her being knocked up."

"You knew Jessie was pregnant?" I asked, toying with a napkin. My leg started to throb.

"Yeah, I told her to go to a clinic to get rid

of it before he found out but she wanted to have it." I knew it.

"You think this guy was a bigwig?" I asked her.

She shrugged. "We get 'em in here all the time, not wanting to be ID'd."

"So no photos of the guy?" I asked, shredding the napkin into little pieces and laying them next to my untouched drink.

"We're not allowed phones on the floor."

"Did Jessie ever talk to you about cutting?" I asked.

Ruby contemplated her glass. "I helped her find the right makeup to cover up her scars. She hadn't cut since she was in middle school she said."

"Did Jessie tell you why she started cutting?" I asked, giving her my best "cop stare." Intimidating but full of concern.

"She said she got interfered with and it messed up her head."

"She say who interfered with her?" I held my breath.

Ruby shook her head. "Never said."

I slid one of my business cards over to her. "Call me if you or any of the girls sees Jessie's customer in here again."

She eyed the card then slipped it into her cleavage and downed her drink in one last gulp.

"The cops better be through in there cuz I gotta lock up for the night." She jumped down from her stool, a little unsteady on her feet. She held out a hand to me. I took it and she helped me down.

"Patty deserved more than this place," I said. "So do you."

"It's too late for either of us," Ruby said. Jacobs and Byron were just coming out of the office. "All done?" she asked them. They both nodded.

"Tell your boss thanks," Byron said.

"Find anything?" I asked.

"Nope, you?" he looked at Ruby still standing by us.

"Nope. Let's go guys. Have a nice night," I said to Ruby. She nodded.

I told Byron what Ruby told me about the guy only using cash and staying hidden in one of the back rooms.

"Get a description of him?" he asked.

"She never saw his face, he went through the back, stayed for a while with Jessie as his lap dancer and left. Every Thursday like clockwork and always at midnight."

"I wish this place had security cameras," he said. Jacobs snorted. "Ruby say anything about Barre and Patty? Any connection there?" Byron asked once we were back outside.

"She didn't know." I lied, hating myself for keeping information from him. They went on their way and I went on mine.

* * *

Two weeks to the day of Jessie's murder and I was no closer to finding Jessie's killer. Cindy was still pissed at me. Byron wasn't too happy with me either when I refused to give up what Ruby told me about Patty. I told him it was an accident and he should stop investigating it. He didn't believe me.

I was also no closer to figuring out how to deal with the pain in my leg. I had to go for an x-ray this afternoon. I downed two pain pills before driving to the clinic. Being at the clinic reminded me of Jessie's incomplete miscarriage. I called Byron and left him a voice mail to remember to canvas the OB/GYN clinics in the area.

After the x-ray I drove to Starbucks. I needed a coffee. My phone rang while I was in line. Several patrons glared at me as I answered. I mouthed, "doctor" to them, that shut them up.

"Dr. Thompson speaking," I said into the phone.

"Since when are you a doctor?" Byron said laughing.

"Just go with it," I said. "What's up?"

"I got your message and yes, I canvassed the clinics and before you ask, no, Jessie wasn't at any of them. Or at least no one matching her description was at them."

"Think she had a miscarriage?" I asked. Several people in line made gasping noises.

"OB," I mouthed again. Heads nodded. It was my turn. "Grande Caramel Macchiato," I said. "One shot of caramel." The barista nodded.

She named the price. I handed her my Visa. She swiped it and handed it back.

"Thanks, I don't need a receipt." I walked over to the area where you picked up your coffee. I leaned against the counter.

"I take it you're at Starbucks," Byron said.

"I needed a coffee after the x-ray, they took forever."

"I forgot about that, when do you get the results?"

"Not sure, probably won't unless something drastic changes."

"Yeah, probably not. You ready to tell me what Ruby said?"

"No. Hang on. My order is up." I nodded to the barista who handed me my cup. I took a sip. *Yes, this is exactly what I need.* I sat down and concentrated on the phone call again. "Anything else going on?"

"I cleared her brothers and her step-daddy of

any abuse."

"So, where are we?"

"We are nowhere, Mel. You are no longer a cop, remember? How many times do I have to remind you?"

"Cindy never did get around to firing me," I said. I fingered the crucifix now hanging around my neck. "Did she tell you we found a crucifix in Jessie's flowerbox?"

"No, is it metal?" I could tell he was getting his hopes up about finding a fingerprint on it.

"Nope, wood. I cleaned it up and I'm wearing it. Cindy gave it to me."

"I don't suppose there's any reason I need it. From what I heard Jessie stopped going to church years ago."

"Oh? I got the impression that she went every Sunday." Now, who told me that? Cindy? I went to Mass every Sunday too. Not something I shared with Byron. I didn't see Jessie there. There were so many masses available she probably picked the late one, I went to the earliest one I could.

"I'll check it out. Look, Mel, I gotta go. Stay away from that AJ character, will ya? He had a bad rep in the military. Seems like he had a difference of opinion with one of his superior officers. Beat him nearly to death."

"Ouch. You sure it's the same guy?"

"Yep, AJ Tanner. They gave him the option of leaving with a medical discharge or prison. He chose discharge."

"Who told you this?" I didn't think the military would.

"AJ seemed proud of it. Told me he changed his ways. In my opinion, leopards rarely change their spots. Warn Cindy away from him too. I don't trust him."

"I could warn Cindy if she was talking to me."

"She's not?"

"She's still mad at me for putting the cops on her boys including her late husband and AJ."

"She'll get over it. Will I see you later on tonight?"

"I don't know, will you?"

"I'll be over around six. Want me to bring takeout?"

"Yes."

"How about ribs and wingdings?" he asked.

"Make sure you get a side of extra coleslaw and extra fries. Oh, and a large order of wings."

"Yes, boss." He hung up. I smiled.

Chapter Eleven

Much to my surprise the spine doc called me two days later.

"I got the results of your x-ray, Mel. It's not good."

"What does that mean?" I asked, sitting down on the sofa.

"The bullet appears to be migrating more toward your spinal cord. Any increase in pain?"

"Yes, but, I attributed it to doing more."

"It's probably from the bullet, I'm looking at the images now. It's not only pressing on the bundle of nerves we call the cauda equina but on the bulging disc too. I'm worried about it. I was hoping it would migrate outward, not inward."

"So, what worries you?" I asked.

"If it continues to migrate you may lose the use of the leg and bladder and bowel control."

Yikes. I bit down on my lower lip hard.

"Now what?"

"I'm afraid the only thing we can do is to try

to remove the bullet. It would help the pain. I could do what's called a laminectomy and shave some of the bone sticking out, relieve that bulging disc too. I'd like you to be admitted tomorrow."

"Tomorrow? As in, Thursday?"

"Yes, the way the bullet is positioned, we really can't wait."

"So, there's no other option?" My hands shook.

"None, sorry. This is my opinion and you're welcome to get another opinion. Don't wait too long though. While you're here we'll do a CT scan too. I have to tell you that the recovery can be painful and long. We're talking six months or longer."

"I thought you said it might be dangerous to remove the bullet, it might cause me to be paralyzed." Not something I wanted to consider.

"I have to provide you with all possible outcomes," he said.

"If I get the surgery and recover completely, no limp, no cane and minimal pain in my back?"

"That's the game plan."

"So, I might be able to go back to being a cop again?"

"I'm not sure you'll be able to pass the annual physical," he hedged.

I laughed. "Oh, I will pass it. Okay, schedule it. What time do I have to be there?"

"Six in the morning."

"Okay. I'll be there."

"Don't drink or eat anything after midnight, meds are okay with sips of water only, no food of any kind."

"Gotcha. See ya tomorrow, doc." I hung up. I debated whether or not to call Byron. I decided not to. He could find out after. I did need to call Cindy though.

"Cindy? Don't hang up. I have to talk to you."

"What do you want?" she asked with a frosty tone. Brr.

"I just wanted you to know that I'm going in for surgery on my back tomorrow. I won't be able to finish the investigation but Byron is still on the case."

"Surgery? For what?" Her voice warmed up.

"The doc wants to remove the bullet. It's migrating closer to my spine." I tried to keep my voice from shaking. I didn't succeed.

"How do you know?" she asked.

"I had an x-ray done on Monday. The doc just called with the results."

"You call Byron?"

I hesitated. "Not yet."

"Good luck tomorrow. I'm sorry, Mel. I have to go." She hung up on me. I put the phone down tears dripping down my chin. Who would be there for me tomorrow? I counted on Cindy for so long, we promised to be there for each other no matter what. I wiped my eyes with the hem of my shirt. On a whim I dialed another number.

"St. Matthew's Parish, how may I help you?"

"Is Father Mark in? Tell him it's Mel Thompson."

"Just a minute, please." A few seconds later

she was back on. "I'll contact you." I heard a click then,

"Hello, Mel, what's going on?"

"I'm going in for surgery tomorrow, Father. Can you come?" As much as I hated to admit it, I said, "I don't have anyone else."

"Of course I can, Mel. What hospital and what time is the surgery?"

"Beechton Hospital. I have to be there at six in the morning."

"I'll stay with you until you go in. Is this for your back?"

"Yes, the recovery can be long. I may be able to go back to the police force after I recover."

"Is that why you are doing the surgery?" he asked.

"No, the doc is recommending it. I guess the bullet is migrating. He said I might be paralyzed if I don't have it or even if I do." My voice shook.

"We'll postpone our dinner on Sunday. I'll get the bishop to extend my post here for a while."

"Thank you, that'd be great. You're a good friend, Mark."

"I'll see you in the morning at the hospital. Stay strong."

"Thanks," I hung up feeling better.

Chapter Twelve

Father Mark greeted me as they wheeled me upstairs to the surgical floor. From there I would be taken to the operating room. A plethora of people came in and out, nurses, aides, an anesthesiologist, my spine doc. At one point they gave me medicine through an IV and I started slurring my words. Father Mark stood right next to me holding my hand the entire time.

I pointed to my bag still sitting on a chair. "Take out necklace," I said. Father Mark rummaged in the bag and pulled out a small box.

"Is this what you want?" I nodded too sleepy to answer. "Want me to open it?" he asked. A nod. He opened it and dropped the box. "Sorry, Mel." He came up from under the bed with the crucifix holding it by the chain.

"Give me," I said. He handed it to me. I clutched it in my hand trying to find comfort in its symbolism.

"It's lovely, where'd you get it?" he asked

as I handed it back to him. He laid it on the bedside table.

"Jessie's. Was Jessie's. Yours?"

"Did I carve it, you mean?" Another nod. He smiled wider. "No, I can't do anything that lovely."

"Cindy said, you gave Jessie." My mind was fogging over. I could barely function.

"If I did, I don't remember."

"At first communion."

"Oh, I gave all the children a crucifix, I order them in batches, this must be one of those. I stopped ordering from that company because the Jesus kept falling off the cross." He grinned. "The only thing left was a plain cross; in one swift movement I turned the children from Catholics to Protestants." He laughed at his joke. I tried to muster a grin. My mouth didn't seem to work right.

"Time to go," a nurse in scrubs with a blue bonnet over her hair said. Another nurse began to unhook me from various tubes and reattach me. I drifted in and out. The bed started moving.

“Wait,” I said. “Can he go?” I pointed to Father Mark who was still in the room.

“No, sorry. You’ll see him in the recovery room. About three hours from now.”

* * *

The only thing I remembered about the operating room was it was cold. I shivered and one of the nurses brought me a warm blanket. I can’t remember if I thanked her or not. I woke up with Father Mark standing over me and something in my nose. I yanked it out and a nurse told me to leave it in. I started to lift my head, a wave of dizziness hit me so I lay back down.

“Last rites?” I asked Father Mark who stood next to me holding a pillow in his hands.

He laughed.“Not exactly. The surgery went well, they said. Your doctor is here to explain it all to you. Want me to leave?”

“No, you can stay.” The doctor had a big smile on his face as he approached the bed.

“We were able to successfully remove the bullet without damaging the nerves, we also removed bone fragments and part of the disc that was bulging out. You should be back to your old self in a few months. Take it slow, no driving for six weeks, no bending or lifting either. I'll have the nurses explain it all to you when you get out of here. For now, I've got you on a pain pump. In a couple of days, once you are able to take in food I'll change it to oral pills. Any questions?"

"Can I have the bullet?"I croaked.

"No, sorry. I gave it to the police, they wanted it." The police? What police? Byron came into view. He had a frown on his face.

"Why didn't you tell me you were having surgery?" he asked with an accusatory tone.

"How'd you find out?" I asked.

"Cindy called me." I'd have to thank Cindy later. I closed my eyes for a moment. When I opened them I was back in my room on the surgical floor. Byron had left.

Father Mark smiled at me."I have to go, Mel. I'm glad you made it through surgery all right. Call me if you need anything." He left too.

The next few days were filled with pain, mostly in my back, the leg pain was minimal. They made me get up and walk around the room. Once I was able to pass gas I could eat again. I think Byron came back for a visit. Something about the bullet. Between the pain medication and the actual pain I didn't get the gist of what he told me.

* * *

Cindy showed up on day five. They were about to discharge me, I had a visiting nurse coming twice a week to help me. Cindy listened to the discharge notes the nurse gave me. She nodded. I tuned them out. I looked out the window instead. The pain was still intense and the narcs they had me on made me loopy. The nurse read through the list of items I brought to make sure I got everything back. I frowned.

"Wait a minute, what about my crucifix? It was lying here on the bedside table. I assumed someone put it in a drawer." The nurse consulted her notes.

"Nothing about a crucifix on my sheet."

"That's because it was in my bag. Father Mark took it out for me. I remember seeing it when I came back from the recovery room."

"You don't mean Jessie's crucifix? The one she got at her First Communion?" Cindy asked. "The one you found in the window box?"

"That's the one."

"You lost it?" Cindy's face scrunched up. "How could you lose it? It was Jessie's." She dabbed at her eyes with a tissue she pulled from her purse. She took a breath. "I'm sure it'll turn up. Can we go now?" she asked the nurse.

"Yes, I'll have the aide bring a wheelchair. Do you understand your medication schedule?"

"Yes, take a pill every two hours, the white ones first, then the yellow ones, then the other smaller white ones and then the bigger white ones if I am in severe pain." The nurse laughed.

"Okay, sign here, and here. Thanks. Hope your recovery at home goes well."

"Thanks for all your help too and thank the other nurses, you were all great."

"I will, 'bye now."

Cindy stood by the door waiting until the aide brought the chair. She wheeled me to the front of the hospital and handed her keys to the Valet Service. They parked your car for you for a fee and then retrieved it once you were done. I waited at the curb until Cindy pulled up in her SUV and the Valet Service woman wheeled me up to the door.

Between the two of us I was able to get in. Cindy got my belongings and we drove off. In silence. Deafening silence. I stared out the window as she drove. Once we were at my condo, she got out to help me step down. In six weeks I could start physical therapy, if I was ready. Until then I had to rest. Byron opened the door for us. He put a hand under my elbow to guide me inside. I sat down on the sofa.

"I thought you couldn't get off," I heard Cindy ask him.

"Just for a few, I gotta get back. Thanks for doing this, Cindy." He shut the door and came back in.

"She isn't going to say goodbye to me?"

Tears fell before I could stop them.

"I'm sorry, Mel. She's still upset about you accusing the boys of abusing Jessie. I think she's putting her grief for Jessie onto you." Yeah, I got that. It still hurt like hell though.

"And before you say no, I've moved back in." He held up a hand to me as I opened my mouth to speak. "It only needs to be temporary if you want. Just until the doc says you can drive. Six weeks, maybe a bit more. I'll be gone most of the day so you can have your space. At night I can help you get undressed, shower, whatever." I shook my head.

"I don't want you to do that, Byron."

"Tough, it's a done deal. I have to go back to the precinct, any requests before I go? Juice? Food? Drugs?"

"Drugs. The yellow ones are due." He took the pills out of the bag from the drugstore.

"When did you get those?"

"I asked the doc to call in the meds to the pharmacy, I picked them up before you got home. Here you go, water or juice?"

"Water is fine." He got me a glass.

"Lay down here, do not climb the stairs. I'll try and be back by four. Here's your phone. Get some rest and I'll see you later. Chinese okay?" I nodded already sleepy. I lay down on the sofa and he covered me with an afghan. He kissed me on the cheek. I barely heard the door click as he left. I meant to ask him about the bullet. Maybe later. If I remembered, that is.

I tried to rally after Byron came in with Chinese, I really did. My attention span was shorter than a fruit fly's at the moment. I took a chopstick full of noodles and half way to my mouth I forgot what I was doing.

"Eat it," Byron prompted.

Oh. I popped it in my mouth, chewed, swallowed and said, "I'm done."

"You only ate a mouthful." I shrugged. I was propped up against pillows he had arranged for me on the couch. I took a sip of the tea.

"Tell me about the bullet," I said trying to keep my eyes open.

"Oh, so you did remember what I said to

you in the hospital. I thought you were too out of it." *Right, I was.* "The ballistics lab found a match. The same gun that shot you also shot Patty Wilcox. I still think Barre is who we need to look at closer."

"Yep." These drugs were making me too sleepy to concentrate. I curled up on my side as instructed by the docs. I let Byron's soothing voice lull me to sleep.

The pain didn't let me sleep all through the night. It never did. I took a white pill and lay back down. I could hear Byron gently snoring upstairs. I smiled. I wished I could go up there and sleep next to him. With a sigh I dragged my laptop over to the couch and balanced it on my lap. I decided to do some searching as long as I was up. I wanted to find a connection between Barre and Jessie and Patty. I mean, other than the obvious one of the two of them working as strippers for him. Why would he have them killed? Were they running drugs for him? Sex trafficking? Prostitution rings? Illegal gambling? Did they see something they weren't supposed to see or hear something they weren't supposed to hear? Was Barre a front for a mob business? Was he money laundering? My thoughts swirled around as I continued to type in names and places.

My search turned up nothing. Nada. Zilch. If I still had access to the database the cops did I might find out more. As far as the Internet was concerned, Barre Enterprises was a legit business. Other than being a sleezy one, that is. My thoughts still swirled as I lay back down.

Chapter Thirteen

I could go upstairs as long as I held onto the railing. The pain in my leg was less. It was still there though. Once I hit the six week mark I could start physical therapy. I looked forward to that day. Byron whistled as he took his morning shower. I grinned. I knew that once he moved in again there would be no way I'd kick him out. And, to tell the truth, I didn't want to. I liked having him here. To hell with being so independent. Maybe it was time I gave in a little. Byron was one of the good ones. I smiled.

"Hey, Williams, you almost done in there?" I asked. I heard the water turn off.

"I'm done. Want to try and take a shower today?" I'd been having what the nurses in the hospital called "a bed bath." It involved washing with this no-rinse soap that made your skin all sticky. No thanks.

"Maybe later tonight. I don't know if I can stand that long." Byron came out with a bright yellow towel wrapped around his waist.

"That's why I got you this," he went into the closet and came out with a box. SHOWER CHAIR, the side of the box read. I burst out in tears. "You don't like it?" Byron asked. He liked to have his presents appreciated, well, who didn't?

"No, it's just that I hate this, all this." I waved my hand around. He came over to the bed and sat down next to me.

"But, it's not forever, Mel. Once you are a bit more recovered I'll take it out and put it in the dumpster, okay?" He kissed the end of my nose. "And maybe we can shower together again." He nuzzled my neck. I pushed him away.

"Don't start something you can't finish, Williams."

"I know, not yet. But, soon." The phone in my hand made me jump. I held it out to Byron.

"I forgot, it's for you. Sherlock called."

He answered it. "Yeah? Speaking. Whatcha got for me, Sherlock?" He listened smiling at me as he nodded to whatever it was she was saying. "Got it, thanks."

"Sherlock is a genius," he said getting dressed in black slacks and a powder blue shirt he tucked into his waistband. God, he looked delicious.

"I'm sure she'd tell you the same thing, what did she want?"

"The bullet from you and from Patty is from Barre's gun. The one registered to him. We can bring him in on this." He kissed me on the cheek before finishing getting dressed. I watched him as he picked out a tie.

"What about Jessie? Is there a connection to Jessie too?"

"No, not yet."

"I told you about Ruby, right?"

"What about her?" he asked buckling his belt. He looked at me. "Don't tell me you talked to her too?"

"I guess with all the surgery stuff I forgot to tell you," I said, averting my eyes. I decided it was time to tell him what she told me.

"I bet, go on," he said, buttoning his shirt.

"She said a customer shot Patty and mine

was random, no connection." He stopped buttoning for a moment digesting the information.

He nodded."I'll get to the bottom of it, Mel. Want some help getting downstairs? Want me to make you a bagel before I leave?"

"No, I'm good. I can maneuver down the stairs on my own. What about you? Gonna get a bagel?"

He shook his head. "I'll catch a bite downtown. Okay, I am out of here. See you tonight. Get some rest." He kissed me on the lips. He hummed as he went down the stairs. Even though he was driving and I wasn't I still kept my bug in the garage. It was vintage. He didn't mind except on the days it was raining. It was already the second week of November. I wondered if I'd be well by Christmas. Probably not. But closer.

I lay down on the bed too tired to go downstairs again. The phone rang. I assumed it would be for Byron.

"Hello?"

"This Mel? Mel the lady cop?" Used to be. *Oh, why bother?*

"Yes."

"This is Ruby, we met down at the club?"

"Ruby, yes, hello." *Funny, I was just talking about her.*

"Look, I heard you had surgery so I know you can't drive yet. But, would you consider coming down here to talk to me? I don't drive either. Alejandro should be at your condo by now." I heard a horn beep outside. I got up and slowly made my way to the window. There was a small black limo idling by the front door.

"He's here but I'm not supposed to travel much yet." I said.

"It's important. You'll want to hear this."

"You can't tell me over the phone?"

"No. Please? And if you could come alone." Now the hairs on the back of my neck were standing up.

"Sure, I'll be there as soon as I can. I have to get dressed first."

"Thanks." She hung up. I knew I wasn't

going to be able to dress in pants. I had a heck of a time getting undies on as it was. I threw a dress on over my head, slipped my feet into Crocs and called it good to go.

On the way out the door I grabbed my cane. I stuffed my wallet and iPhone in my dress pocket. I grabbed a jacket too. Although we didn't have snow yet, the mornings were cold.

I knocked on the limo window. Alejandro got out and opened the limo door for me.

"Thanks, good morning," I said. He nodded. I had taken my pain pills so the pain was at a minimum.

In a few minutes we were at The Barre. Alejandro opened the door for me and held out a hand. I took it. I gingerly made my way to the club door using my cane for support. He opened it with a key. I walked in. The same dingy lighting and the same stale smells greeted me.

I spotted Ruby sitting in the corner of the bar in one of the easy chairs. As I got closer I realized she was hooked up to an oxygen tank. She pointed to it as I sat down on the edge of the chair.

“You see why it was easier for you to come to me? This thing is a real bitch to haul around.” She gestured to the bar. “Want something to drink?”

“I’m fine, Ruby. Why did you want me to come and see you?”

“I heard that the bullets between you and Patty matched.” My, news travels fast.

“And?” I wasn’t going to give anything away.

“Remember I told you a customer shot Patty?” I nodded. “I lied about that.” I waited. She looked around the room. “You know I never did much with my life, ‘cept this club. Barre and me used to be an item back in the day. Doc says I’ve gotta go to one of them dying homes? Where you go in and you don’t come out?”

“Hospice?”

“Yeah, hospice. I’m moving in today. Got my stuff already packed. Alejandro’s gonna drive me. Don’t expect I’ll get too many visitors in there. Probably won’t last the month out.

Would've liked to have seen another Christmas though." She laughed. "Not that it would matter, Santie hasn't brought me presents since I was tiny." She took a couple of deep breaths breathing in the oxygen. I waited.

"I wanted to confess something to you. You can tell your cop boyfriend if you want."

"Okay, what?" What was she going to tell me? Was she going to tell me that Barre had Patty killed? I looked around the club with a nervous glance. Where was Barre? Was he lurking in the shadows to kill me? I swallowed wishing I hadn't come down here alone.

"I did it," she said. My head snapped back to look her in the eye. She sat back in her chair as if she was relieved.

"Did what?" I asked. I made myself comfortable, well, as comfortable as I could.

"I shot you, I shot Patty. I used Barre's gun. The one he keeps in his safe."

"What? Why?"

"Well, you told Jessie to get out of the business. We already had her scheduled for two more films. She made more money for us than all the girls here. I was pissed at you so I shot you." She was so matter of fact about it. "And, as long as I'm confessing, I killed Patty too." She closed her eyes. "Patty got it in her head she didn't need us any longer. She was going to leave Barre. She was one of our top dancers. She said she was going to take her boy and raise him in the country. Like she'd make it in the country. Hah." She opened her eyes. "I told her either stay with us or face the consequences, she laughed in my face. Said she wasn't going to let some old, bald, junkie tell her what to do anymore. She said one of the guys at the club was going to pay her to be his full-time maid at his country estate. She was the stupid one. He wanted a full-time hooker at his disposal, that's what he wanted. I told her so. She got pissed at me when he backed out of the deal. I told him to take one of the younger girls instead and he thought it was a better idea so he asked Renee to go instead. Patty came at with a knife, I had to defend myself. I shot her. Right between the eyes. Serves her right for trying to leave us in the lurch that way." She turned her gaze to me. "Go ahead and call your cop now. I won't live long enough to go to prison anyways."

"I wish you hadn't told me, Ruby. I liked you."

"Yeah, I have that effect on people. At first they love me, then later on, not so much." Especially if they find out you tried to have them killed. She started coughing and it took her a while to catch her breath. "Some kind of pneumonia," she said. She motioned to Alejandro who was hovering near us. "The detective is ready to go. Thanks for listening," she said leaning back in her chair. I got up. What was there to say?

* * *

Byron came home at six. I rested on the couch.

He frowned at me. "I heard you visited Ruby down at Barre today. Should I count off the ways that was jeopardizing your health?" I ignored that question.

"Is Alejandro an informant?" I asked. My eyes widened as Byron grinned. "He is, isn't he? I should've guessed. I suppose he told you all about my chat with her."

"He did. Guess I don't have to keep investigating Patty's murder or your shooting."

"Do you believe Ruby?" I asked him. "She could be covering up for Barre."

"Even if she is, we'll never know. I brought him in for questioning, as far as he knows the gun is still in his safe. He did say that only he and Ruby knew the combination though. The only fingerprints on the gun belong to Ruby. Barre said he hasn't shot it in years."

"Ah."

"You seem pretty subdued considering you found out who shot you and why."

"It seems, oh, I don't know, understated. I wanted it to be a bigger reason why someone would shoot another human being. Instead of she was pissed off at me for losing her cash cow?" I shook my head.

"You know that people shoot other people

for stupid reasons, Mel. Remember that guy that shot the other guy for his shoes?" I nodded. "Or the woman who got shot because she refused to move out of the way?"

"But those people aren't me," I said. "I'm a cop or was."

"You're not invincible, Mel. And you don't have magical powers, none of us do. Even good cops get shot."

"Yeah." I wasn't convinced. "There's still Jessie. Think that Barre or Ruby orchestrated that too?"

He shrugged. "I don't know, Mel." I didn't either.

Chapter Fourteen

Cindy called. I was, as they say, over the moon. She was on her way over. She had something to tell me. Something important.

She brought us Starbucks. Be still my beating heart. She gave me a tentative hug.

"How are you feeling?" she asked walking into the dining room. She put the coffees on the table. I followed the coffee.

I picked one up. "Macchiato?" I asked. She nodded. "I'm doing better, thanks. How are you doing?"

"Okay, I guess. AJ helped me clean out Jessie's place. I gave most of it to the resale shop. I have her computer with her photo's on it. AJ said he'd print them out if I wanted. Would you like some copies?" I wished I had taken the Hello Kitty bag the first time we were there.

I sat down sipping the coffee. Cindy sat down across from me. "Sure, if you want." I looked at her. She looked away. "So, what's your news?"

She turned back to me. "You aren't going to like it."

"What is it?" I took a bigger drink. What was she going to tell me? I felt scared that she was going to tell me that she no longer wanted to be friends. The coffee turned sour in my stomach.

"I'm pregnant, isn't that great?" To say I was stunned would be the understatement of the year.

"Pregnant? I didn't know you were dating anyone." She used to tell me everything. Her news made me sad. Not sad that she was pregnant. Sad that she hadn't told me the minute the stick turned blue.

"I'm not, really."

"Well, unless you tell me your name is Mary, I doubt you could be pregnant unless you are dating or at least having great sex."

She laughed running her hands through her cropped hair. That was new too. She was a whole new Cindy. I worried. "Tell me about it," I said.

"If you haven't guessed by now, it's AJ and he is so happy for us." Us? When did AJ become an "us?"

"You and AJ are back together?" I asked in as neutral a tone as I could muster.

She giggled. She actually giggled. "Yes, we are. He moved in last week. We're making wedding plans, Mel. I am so happy." Her eyes twinkled. I hated to be a wet blanket but…

"You remember he hit you, right? That's why you divorced him in the first place?" Something clicked. "Wait, how far along are you? You can't be pregnant with AJ's kid, he's only been back a month."

"He's been back for six weeks and before that he was in town last month to find a place to live before he moved here permanently."

"Oh, so you slept with him two months ago? And you didn't tell me?"

"I knew you'd be like this, Mel. I knew it. You never liked AJ."

"That's not true, Cin. I didn't like the way he treated you, that's all."

"You pushed me into divorcing him. You said I'd be better off without him and I haven't been. Oh, sure for a few years I was happy with Justin and I got Jessie from that marriage. After Justin died I felt so lonely, so alone. The kids were all grown up and moved away. I missed being part of a couple."

"I know, Cin. Me too."

"You have Byron. I had no one. Why do you care so much who I sleep with? This is my last chance at happiness, don't you see that? I'll be forty next year. I won't be able to have any more babies soon. I know this baby won't replace Jessie, but it's another chance for me and AJ."

"Does he promise not to hit you again?"

"Give it a rest, Mel. It was over twenty years ago! He's a changed man."

"Do changed men beat up their superior officers so bad they end up in the Intensive Care Unit?"

She stared at me. "What are you talking about?"

"Ask AJ why he got out of the military. He

beat up his officer and they told him either get out or go to jail. He got out." Cindy began to shake her head before I was done speaking.

"No, I don't believe you; you want to turn me against him. Well, it's not going to happen this time. AJ and I are together and I am having this baby. I was hoping you'd stand up for me at the wedding…"

"Oh, Cindy, please just think about this? Give it a year before you marry him again? That's what all the grief books say; don't make any big decisions for a year."

"I wish you could hear yourself sometimes," she said. "Can't you see that this marriage will help me get over Jessie's death?" She began to cry. "I wish you'd be happy for me."

I put a hand over her hand. "I am happy for you."

She sniffed. "I can't wait a year. We want to be married before the baby comes. You'll stand up with me?"

"If I can stand, when is it?"

"When we can get all the kids here. Their

schedules are so erratic."

"Do they know about the baby yet?"

"No, not yet. I wanted to wait until after the wedding."

"Promise me that if AJ lays one hand on you or the baby you'll tell me?"

"Okay." She held up her hand in the Girl Scout's salute. "I promise, On my honor as a Girl Scout." We both laughed. The tension was eased somewhat. I still felt worried for her.

I waited until I knew Cindy was gone for the day. I called her number, AJ answered.

"AJ? Hi, It's Mel."

"Mel! Good to hear your voice. Cindy told me she was going to give you our good news."

"Yes, she did. That's what I wanted to talk to you about."

"Yeah?" He sounded relaxed.

I made my voice casual. "Yeah, I just wanted to tell you that if you ever lay a hand on Cindy or anyone of her kids, you'll have me to deal with. Remember what I told that scumbag Barre? Well, the same goes for you."

“What, you gonna spray me with your Glade?”

“I mean it, AJ.”

“I know you do, Mel. But, I’ve changed. I promise you.”

“A leopard doesn’t change its spots,” I said copying Byron.

“Give it a rest, Mel. She’s counting on you to help her through this motherhood thing again.”

“I’ll help her. Just remember what I said. And you should also remember, I have a cop boyfriend and he has a very big gun. Bigger than yours.” AJ guffawed then hung up. I hoped that Cindy was right, that AJ had changed. I doubted he had. I guess I should give him a break for Cindy’s sake and for the baby’s sake. My insides churned with dread thinking what he might do to her if he got angry with her.

Chapter Fifteen

I knew I was pushing myself by starting physical therapy on my own. I began to do some back strengthening exercises. At first the pain was intense. I tried taking pain pills before the exercises. Eventually the pain stopped hurting. I wanted to walk but the sidewalks were too icy.

“It’s almost Thanksgiving,” Byron said. He was making us dinner. A stir-fry with vegetables and chicken. I sat at the table watching him. I helped out by chopping the veggies.

“Yeah, so? Want to have a turkey?”

“Sure, but my mom called. She wants us to go to her house. It’s only a two hour drive.”

“No, I can’t.”

“Why not?” he asked. He threw in a handful of peanuts into the wok.

“She hates me,” I said.

He laughed. “True, but she invited you too.”

“No, I’m not going to be scrutinized by your

relatives. Everyone is going to wonder why you are with me. Again."

"Why would they wonder that?" he said taking the veggies and putting them in the wok. They hissed and he stirred them.

"Come on, Byron. Your mom was ecstatic when you broke up with me, don't deny it."

"I don't. But, she's going to have to deal with it. We're together now and will be in the future."

"Yeah? You got a crystal ball, Williams?"

"I don't need one. I'll call mom tomorrow and let her know we can't come. Maybe for Christmas?"

"Maybe," I said. "It all depends on how I feel." Now she has another reason to hate me, I won't let her baby boy come home for Thanksgiving. I sighed.

"Fair enough. Let's eat. Mind if I have a beer?" he asked, dishing up two plates. It smelled delicious. I was beginning to get my appetite back, a good sign, I thought.

"Go ahead. Give me a soda, please." He

served us and for a few minutes neither one of us had much to say. The food was good.

"Can we go to church on Sunday?" Byron asked.

"Why?"

"Just cuz."

I shrugged. "Maybe. Is there an ulterior motive here?"

"Nope, just miss going is all." He smiled.

"Which church?" I asked.

"St. Matthew's. It's the prettiest with all those stained glass windows in the front."

"So, let me get this straight. You want to go to church because you miss seeing the windows?"

"Something like that." Why did I have my suspicions about this? What's he up to?

"There better not be a ring involved with this going to church thing," I said, stabbing at a piece of broccoli with a chopstick.

"What kind of a ring?" he asked, frowning. *AHA! I knew it.*

"No rings, Byron. I mean it."

"You mean, right now? Or never?" he asked, frowning at me.

"Never is a long time," I said, eating some rice. "And, that's all I am saying on the subject." He frowned again. I didn't enlighten him that I was going to Mass or had been before the surgery. Maybe we could go on Sunday. I could light a candle for Jessie, Patty and for Ruby.

We were in the middle of watching a movie when my phone rang. I picked it up.

"Hello?"

"May I speak to a Detective Thompson?"

"Speaking, who is this?"

"Oh, hello. My name is Betty Burke, I'm one of the nurses at EverPlace. I've been taking care of Ruby Barre." Ruby Barre? She and Barre were married?

"Yes."

"She gave me your name and number and asked me to call you. The doctor thinks she doesn't have long and she wanted to see you one last time. Can you come tonight?"

"Now?" I glanced outside. The snow the

weatherman predicted was beginning to fall.

"Yes, I'm afraid she doesn't have too much time left. Can I tell her you are on your way?"

"Yes, I'm on my way." I hung up.

"You're on your way where?" Byron asked, sitting up.

"It's Ruby, she's dying. She wants to see me before she does. That was a nurse from the hospice. Can you drive me or should I call a cab?"

"I'll drive if you are sure you want to go. This is the woman who shot you."

"I remember. Let's go, help me with my boots, please. I'll need my cane too."

In a few minutes we were headed down Main Street. The snow fell lightly around us enveloping us in a cocoon of white. Byron turned down a side road and pulled up in front of a modern looking building.

"I'll help you in and go park the car. Wait for me at the front desk." I nodded. He left the car running as he helped me negotiate the short walk inside. We rang the bell. A woman opened it. She was dressed in blue scrubs with short cropped red hair, and I mean, red Lucille Ball color hair. Her hazel eyes were friendly and she smiled at us.

"Detective Thompson? And you must be Detective Williams? She said you'd probably come too. Right this way."

"I have to go park the car," Byron said ducking back out. The nurse nodded.

"Want to wait here for him to return?" she asked me.

I shook my head. "No, let's go to Ruby's room." I stamped the snow off my boots with my cane as best I could. She led the way down a hall and stopped in front of a room. She gestured with her arm.

"This is Ruby's room. Let me tell her you are here." I nodded. She went inside. I hung just outside. I could hear her. "Ruby? Wake up, Ruby. Detective Thompson is here to see you, want her to come in?" A voice whispered but I couldn't hear what the voice said. Betty came back to the doorway and crooked her finger at me. "Come in. There's a button by the bed if you need me. I'll show the other detective in." I nodded. She didn't seem too surprised that one of her patients wanted to see two detectives—well, one—late at night. Maybe it wasn't too odd a happening here. Deathbed confessions and all that.

I walked in. Ruby lay in a bed covered in a pink quilt decorated with roses. The room was done in pinks with a rose pink border that split the room down the middle. A small lamp with a pink lampshade sat on a nightstand next to the bed. It was the only illumination. A rocking chair with a matching ottoman sat in the corner of the room near a window. If I didn't know I was in a hospice I could've been at a Bed and Breakfast, it was decorated in a similar style. I walked up to the bed. Ruby opened her eyes.

"Hello, Ruby, it's Mel."

"Mel? I'm glad you came." She was hooked up to oxygen, the tubing ran to the wall.

"Byron is here too, he's parking the car. I told him what you said about me and Patty." I wasn't sure if the walls here had ears or not so I was being discreet. She smiled. Her face much thinner than the last time I saw her. Her hand crabbed the quilt and I grabbed it squeezing it.

"How come you didn't tell me you and Barre were married?"

"Didn't think it mattered. Still love him though."

"Does he know you're in bad shape?"

She nodded. "Was here earlier. I told him to go home. He said he'd see me tomorrow. Won't."

Byron chose that moment to walk in. He strode over to the bed. "Hey, Ruby, how's it going?"

She seemed to rally a little for him. "Not good but better now that you are here," she said attempting to flirt.

He laughed. "Well, it's good to see you again. I'm here if you need me." He went over to the rocking chair and sat down nodding at me. I know he'd give me the chair in an instant if I wanted it. I continued to squeeze Ruby's hand.

"I'm not sure why you wanted me here, Ruby. If you want me to forgive you, I do."

She shook her head slightly. "Not necessary. Look in drawer." I opened the top drawer of her bedside table. I saw a bible so I pulled it out.

"You want me to have your bible?" Me?

"Open it," she said, sounding weaker. "Paper inside." I opened it and a paper with the words LAST WILL AND TESTAMENT fell out. I unfolded it and cleared my throat. I read aloud.

"I, Ruby Barre do hereby leave my half of the club, BARRE to Detective Mel Thompson to do with as she pleases." It was signed by several hospice workers, including her nurse. I saw Barre's signature too. A notary had stamped a seal on it.

"Ruby, you don't have to do this. I'm going to be fine."

"Can't work as a cop cuz of me, wanted to do something." She closed her eyes. I started to let go of her hand but she opened them again. "Left the other half to Patty's boy. Barre agreed."

"You can give it all to Patty's boy, Ruby. I won't mind."

She shook her head slightly. "Half yours, half his. Sell it. Worth a bundle. Lawyer will call you."

"Thank you, Ruby. I wish I had known you back in the day."

She smiled again. "Back when I had hair? Hellion," she said. I had no doubt of that. The nurse reappeared.

"All finished Ruby? These nice people need to get going, it's a blizzard out there. The first snow of the season."

Ruby let go of my hand. "Finished. Thanks for forgiving." She said to me. "Take paper with you." I handed it to Byron who put it in his coat pocket. I bent down and kissed her cheek.

"Thanks for being my friend, Ruby. I bet when you go to wherever you are headed your hair will be full and long and red again."

"Just like mine," Betty the nurse joked.

"G'night," I said to Ruby who nodded.

Byron took my elbow steering me out. Neither one of us said a word.

"Wait here until I get the car cleaned off. I'll be right back." There were chairs in the lobby. I sat down. The nurse did not reappear. I felt tears forming and I swallowed hard to keep them at bay. I heard tires crunching on snow. I got up. Byron. He came to the door just as I opened it. "Watch the sidewalk, it's getting icy." I let him lead me to the car. I lay back against the seat as soon as I buckled my seat belt, my cane next to me. I dozed off as Byron drove us slowly home. I woke up once we were at the condo.

Again, Byron helped me inside. I lay on the couch, too tired to manage the stairs tonight. He covered me up and brought me my nighttime pain pills. I leaned on one elbow as I sat up to take the pills.

The phone rang. Byron picked it up before the second ring. He walked into the kitchen with it speaking quietly into the phone. He came back in looking sad.

"Ruby is gone, she passed right after we left.

That was her nurse." I nodded letting the sadness wash over me. Poor Ruby.

"Guess I'm the part owner of a strip club," I said.

"Guess so. Free lap dances included in ownership?" he asked. I knew he was trying to make me feel better.

"As soon as I can lap dance, you'll be the first to know."

* * *

Byron bought us a turkey. He invited Sherlock and Karen over to share it with us. They accepted and brought a movie about a dysfunctional family during the holidays. I laughed so hard when Karen said, "it's a collection of stories based on my family at the holidays."

The phone rang. Byron's mom. He put it on speaker for me to hear.

"Say hi to Mel, mom, you're on speaker phone."

"Now why would you do that? Take it off right now!" I smiled at Sherlock who raised an eyebrow at me. Byron took the phone into the other room.

"Byron's mom doesn't like me," I said.

Sherlock shrugged. "Karen's mom thinks I am the devil's spawn."

"No, she doesn't," Karen said. "She thinks you are the devil himself. She asked me to check under your hairline for the 666 number."

"She did not," Sherlock said.

"She did, I swear. I told her you must've had it removed because all I found was a small scar near your hairline."

"I told you I fell off a swing when I was five."

"So you say," Karen said, winking at me. Their easy demeanor with each other made me envious. Would Byron and I ever be that easy with one another?

Byron came back into the room. "Mom says, Happy Thanksgiving, Mel." I looked at Karen and she looked at Sherlock. The three of us guffawed. "What did I miss?" Byron asked.

Chapter Sixteen

The Sunday after Thanksgiving was my farewell dinner with Father Mark. I'd miss him. I understood he postponed his new post in Ireland to wait for me to recover more. His new parish wanted him installed before Christmas so he could do a midnight Christmas Eve mass. I envied them, Father Mark did a wonderful rendering of the birth of Christ, quite dramatic. I often joked he should've been an actor instead of a priest.

I wore my good linen slacks along with a chocolate brown blouse. I would be sad to see him go. I was glad he waited until I was more recovered though. Eight weeks since Jessie's murder. I was finally able to schedule Physical Therapy and had my first appointment this coming week. I could drive now too. My leg still hurt but not like before the surgery.

Mille opened the door with her coat on. I raised my eyebrows at her. "Family emergency," she explained as she headed out the door. I hesitated not sure if I should go in or not. Mark came up to the door to greet me. "Come on in, Mel, Millie has left a great dinner for us." I went in. He smiled at me. "You look nice tonight, hot date?"

I laughed. "Yeah, with this guy who is so ugly I cringe every time I look at him." I made a beeline for the nearest chair, leaning my cane against the side.

He laughed and handed me a drink. "White wine I believe?" I hesitated for half a second. To heck with the pain meds. A small glass of white wine wouldn't hurt me.

"Yes, thanks." I took a sip. It was dry and sweet. "It's good."

He nodded. "Millie made mussels fried in butter, along with steamed clams; a fresh green salad with bleu cheese dressing and chocolate cake for dessert," he said.

"Wow, I can feel my arteries hardening as I speak."

"Yeah, Millie doesn't believe in what she

calls 'tasteless' meals or cooking without lots and lots of butter."

"It smells delicious," I said.

"We might as well eat while it is hot," Mark said, standing up. I stood up too and reached for my cane.

Mark shook his head. "Leave it, you can lean on me." He offered me his arm. Grateful for his support, I nodded letting him lead me to the dining room. He helped me into a chair before sitting.

In the center of the table was a big bowl of salad. Mark took the salad tongs and put some on my salad plate. Fresh, red cherry tomatoes, cucumbers, shredded carrots. ripe olives, walnuts, avocado slices, arugula and leaf lettuce topped with bleu cheese dressing, feta cheese, and what looked like homemade croutons made a mound in front of me.

I sighed with contentment. "I won't be able to eat all this. It's looks delicious though. Did Millie make the croutons?"

"She doesn't use any store-bought ones. She

also made the dressing."

I dug in. The dressing was sharp, tangy and better than any store-bought dressing I ever had. I think I moaned at how good it was. Mark laughed.

We both polished off our salads. I didn't think I could eat it all. My appetite was definitely back.

Mark went over to the stove and brought back a covered dish. He unveiled it. "Clams and mussels sautéed in garlic butter with fresh mushrooms."

"Would you believe I've never tried mussels?" I asked, taking a spoonful of them, along with a couple of clams. "I like clams in chowder, can't say I'm a big fan of them otherwise."

"You're not going to make me tell Millie you didn't eat any of her dinner now, are you?" Mark said with a teasing tone.

"I'll eat them," I said, taking a bite of a mussel. I made a face. "Bitter." I pointed to his plate, his only held clams. "No mussels?"

Now it was his turn to make a face. “I don’t like them but go ahead and eat as much as you like. I have these flown in from Alaska. Father Paul wants me to cook them when he visits. Well at least you tried one,” Mark said. “Maybe a bite of another one will change your mind. It is an acquired taste.”

I stabbed another one with my fork and nibbled on the end of it. “Yuck,” I said putting my fork down. “It’s definite. I don’t like mussels.” I ate the clams on my plate. I didn’t ask for more. Mark got up to get more wine and caught the edge of his hand on the mussels/clams dish and it went flying onto the floor.

“Oh, no,” I said, staring down at the mess.

“I’ll clean it up,” Mark said. “Sorry you don’t get seconds.” He bustled around mopping it up.

“I didn’t really want seconds, the salad filled me up,” I said.

After he wiped up the spill, he poured us more wine and brought out the chocolate cake.

He looked at me with an expectant expression. "How big of a piece do you want?"

I groaned and gestured with my thumb and forefinger. "Small." He cut me a bigger piece and added a scoop of vanilla ice cream next to it.

I ate all of it. He watched me with an amused look. He had a small piece on his plate he ate with gusto.

"Coffee in the parlor?" he asked. I nodded looking around for my cane forgetting I left it next to the easy chair. "I'll get your cane," Mark said. He brought it to me and when I reached for it, he set it against the wall. "Let me help you again."

Feeling warm, contented and full, we went back to the parlor where a roaring fire blazed in the fireplace. I was beginning to feel sleepy from all the food.

"I am stuffed," I said, wishing I had on sweat pants that would allow my waist to expand rather than the buttoned pants I did have on.

"Millie is a great cook," Mark said once we both had our coffees, he put a shot of Irish

Whiskey in both along with a dollop of whipped cream. “It’s okay to kick your shoes off and relax, Mel.”

I nodded kicking my shoes off and tucking my feet under me on the sofa. One of my shoes went partway under so I bent down to move it back out. The crucifix lay under the couch. My crucifix. Or rather Jessie’s crucifix. I pulled it out holding it up.

“This is mine, the one I lost in the hospital, how did it get here?”

“Are you sure it’s yours?”

“Yes, when I cleaned it off, there was a tiny chip near the top, this one has the same chip.” I stared at Father Mark. He frowned then smiled.

“I remember, you had it in the hospital during your surgery, right?”

“Yes, but it disappeared.”

“I took it so it wouldn’t get stolen. I was planning on giving it back to you as soon as you returned home.”

“Why didn’t you?”

“I misplaced it. I couldn’t find it anywhere.

It must've dropped under the couch. Millie's eyes aren't as good as they used to be. I doubt she even cleans under there. I'm sorry, Mel, it must've slipped my mind." I shrugged putting it around my neck and tucking it inside my blouse. At least Cindy will be happy I found it.

"Should I get going?" I asked untucking my legs and preparing to stand up.

"No, no. Stay and enjoy your coffee." I glanced out the window. The snow was coming down quite hard.

I gestured to it. "It's snowing and driving in it not to mention walking in it, is treacherous with my cane."

"You're welcome to use the spare room for the night. My flight doesn't leave until tomorrow morning. If the roads are bad I could have my rideshare driver drop you at your condo first and you could pick up your car once the roads clear." It was a good solution. I'd stayed at the rectory before when I stayed too late.

"If you're sure I won't be in the way," I said. I should text Byron to let him know where I am. He drove to his mother's to visit her for the weekend and wasn't planning on coming home until tomorrow.

"It's not a problem, unless you'd like to call Byron to come and get you," he said.

"Can't, he went to his mother's for the weekend. He's not coming back until tomorrow," I said, settling back against the sofa cushions and yawning.

"Speaking of Jessie, how's the investigation going into Jessie's death?" he asked.

"Not good. The leads haven't panned out. The missing piece is still who Jessie was meeting on top of that building. Whoever it was must've been desperate to push her off of it." I paused. "Of course no one really knows what they would do in a desperate situation until they are in that situation, do they?"

"No, they don't." He got up again. "Excuse me but I forgot to check my blood sugar after dinner. Should I do it here or I can go into the bathroom, I know it makes some people squeamish."

"It doesn't bother me any. I didn't know you were a diabetic, Mark."

"Have been since I was a kid. As long as I check my blood sugar and adjust my insulin dose I'm fine."

My brain was fuzzy. I looked at the coffee in my hand. "I think I've had too much to drink," I said. I heard my words begin to slur. "I feel woozy." I laughed. "If woozy is a word." I ran my tongue over my lips. "And my lips are tingling." I rubbed the back of my neck. "I seem to be getting a migraine too." Guess I shouldn't have mixed pain meds with alcohol after all.

"You can stay here on the couch if you like; it pulls out into a sofa bed or you can use the spare room if you need to lay down." Mark stood.

I got up. The room began to spin. "No, I better…I mean I better…" The room spun around me. I felt myself falling right before I blacked out.

I woke up in a darkened room. Someone was standing over me. I yelped. "It's just me,

Mark," Mark said.

"What happened?" I tried to sit up but he pushed me back down. "What's going on, Mark? Where am I?"

"You're on the third floor of the rectory. It hasn't been used in years until recently." He lit a small lamp sitting on the nightstand. I blinked in the dim light but at least my head wasn't swimming any longer. "I don't feel well," I said. "I feel like I might be allergic to something I ate. My face feels numb." I raised my hands to my face and touched it. I noticed my words were beginning to slur again. "I think I should go to the ER, I really don't feel well."

"No, you are fine here," Mark said.

"Please call 911 for me, Mark. I'm sick." And before I could stop myself I threw up the dinner I had just eaten. Mark jumped up away from it in time. I lay back. "I'm sorry, Mark. Please. I feel so sick."

He stood by the door. "You just couldn't let it be, could you?"

"What? What are you talking about? Call

911." I tried to raise my head but couldn't. The sick smell was making me want to throw up again. I tried to hold it in but couldn't.

Mark walked over and handed me a wastebasket. "Throw up in here. This won't last much longer."

"Why? What do I have?" My brain was fuzzy but I couldn't understand why he wasn't calling 911 for me. I looked at the nightstand for my phone but it wasn't there. It must still be downstairs. I doubted I would be able to make it down the stairs to get it. I felt so weak. I noticed that my breathing had become shallower.

"You have what is known as PSP, or Paralytic Shellfish Poisoning. The mussels are contaminated with it." He seemed so calm. "I, of course, didn't eat any of them. You were supposed to eat several. I only hope that one bite does what it is supposed to do. A milligram can kill you."

"What is it supposed to do to me?" I said, slurring the words not sure I heard him right. My lips, tongue and gums were numb. "Kill me?"

"Exactly."

"Why, Mark?" He fingered the crucifix that was now around his neck. My crucifix or rather Jessie's. He must've taken it off me when I was unconsciousness. I wonder if he gave me something to knock me out.

"How long?" I asked.

"Not long, a few hours perhaps. Jessie ate a whole plateful so by the time we were finished with dinner she was already feeling the effects." He laughed. "Of course the mussels on top of the alprazolam I gave her helped to make her even more unsteady."

Even through my brain fuzz I heard what he had said. "You killed Jessie? Why?"

He laughed. "We had an affair Mel. I met her at the strip club where she worked. Every Thursday at midnight. Of course we'd already been sleeping together by then. She came onto me when she was in middle school." He laughed. "Imagine, little Jessie Lewis so full of love for her priest. We kept it going all through high school and I'm the one who suggested she work at Barre. Barre and I are good friends. He gets me any girl I want but once Jessie started working there, she was the only one I wanted." He stared down at the crucifix. "She promised me she wouldn't get pregnant but she did." He laughed. "She said she wanted to keep it. She wanted me to leave the priesthood and marry her. I couldn't do that. I have ambitions; I want to be a bishop someday, a cardinal. I told her I wasn't going to give up on being a priest. She went ballistic on me. Threatened to go to the bishop and expose me. She said she'd tell him I seduced her when she was a child. I couldn't let her destroy me that way. I told her I'd pay for her to go away, wherever she wanted to live until the baby was born and then arrange to have a couple adopt it. She refused." My head was beginning to hurt more. The tingling turned into burning and now even my toes burned. I thrashed around on the bed trying to get rid of the searing pain. It was no use, the pain was becoming more intense. Mark looked at me. "Jessie refused to listen to me. I didn't know what to do so I persuaded her to meet me on the roof of the Tower Building for a romantic dinner for two."

"Please help me, Mark, please," I begged. He ignored me continuing on with his story.

"Then after she ate the contaminated mussels she began to get short of breath. I told her that I was leaving for Ireland and that I was going to be in charge of a larger congregation. I told her she was not welcome to come with me and that I didn't want her anymore." He laughed here. "If you want the truth, she was too old for me. I wasn't attracted to her anymore."

"You gave her the crucifix when she was only thirteen," I said, slurring the words even more.

"I did, it was her gift for allowing me to love her. She was such a pretty child. So sweet. At first she cried complaining that it hurt. I tried to be gentle with her. Eventually she looked forward to our meetings after church, she got as much out of it as I did. More in fact. I tired of her though. She got so needy, always wanting more from me. I ended it once when she was in high school but she begged me to take her back, so I did. When I found out she was stripping at Barre I went to see her. She was so lovely up there. I wanted her to leave Barre, I told her that if she did I'd always love her and she'd be my forever girl." He laughed again. I was having trouble focusing.

"On the roof she started crying and sobbing. Making a racket. She clawed at me when her breathing got worse. Begging me to take her with me we could raise the baby in Ireland. I watched her as she clutched at her throat trying to get a breath." He stepped closer to me. "I didn't mean to kill her. She came at me with her hands extended in claws. I grabbed her hands to steady her, she walked backwards toward the edge crying and sobbing. I kept telling her to calm down. I let go of her hands and she stepped backwards into nothing. She fell. I raced down but she was dead. I gave her last rites and then cleaned up the dinner." He looked at me. "Are you having trouble breathing? You see PSP kills you by giving you respiratory arrest. You are starved for oxygen and eventually you die." He snapped his fingers. "I did enjoy being with Jessie but I couldn't let her destroy me, Mel, surely you see that?" He sighed. "I made the mistake of giving her this." He fingered the crucifix. "I broke into her place after she died to get it back but I couldn't find it. I searched your condo too. I thought maybe she sold it or lost it. I know she wasn't wearing it when she died. I thought I was in the clear." He sighed again. The room was getting dimmer and my breathing was shallower. A gray haze seemed to surround me and I felt as if I was floating above myself.

"Then you showed up with this at the hospital and I knew it was a matter of time before you put it together. Once you're dead, I'll call 911 and tell them you had an allergic reaction to the clams. The mussels will be in the garbage disposal by then. It will be sad for everyone, first you get shot in the line of duty, then your best friend's daughter dies, then you die. Sad and tragic." He drew himself up to his full height. "I'll leave for Ireland in two weeks after your memorial service and will be on my way to getting everything I want."

"Not exactly," said a voice behind him. An overhead light was switched on. The intense light felt like someone was stabbing me in my head and eyes. I blinked trying to focus. There stood Byron and Don Jacobs both with guns drawn on Mark. He looked wildly at them then at me. Byron talked into his shoulder mic. "Need a bus at St. Matt's rectory and hurry."

"Turn around pretty boy," Jacobs said to Mark. He clapped handcuffs on Mark. "You are under arrest for the murder of Jessie Lewis and the attempted murder of Mel Thompson. You have the right to remain silent…" I tried to focus on Byron's face above me as he was saying something but it was too difficult to breathe. The room spun again and I floated higher toward the ceiling. *Odd sensation. Am I dead?*

I woke up in a hospital room with an oxygen mask on me. I tried to take it off but a voice told me to "leave it on." I opened my eyes and in a chair next to my bed sat Byron. A nurse was adjusting the oxygen level. I tried to sit up but decided against it.

"What happened?" I asked.

"Father Mark poisoned you," Byron said coming over to stand next to me. He grasped my hand in his. "It was touch and go for a while but the docs think you are on the road to recovery."

"How long have I been here?" I looked around.

"Two days. The toxin almost killed you, Mel," Byron looked down at me. Were those tears in his eyes? I squeezed his hand back.

"How did you find me, I mean how did you know it was Mark?"

"Sherlock called and said she found a biotoxin in Jessie's system. Something called saxitoxin. Caused by eating shellfish of some kind. It's what killed her."

"But what about Mark?" I asked. I pointed to a water cup on the bedside table and he handed it to me. I took a grateful sip. It tasted cold, sweet and like nectar. I took another drink.

"Good," I said. I handed it back to Byron. I

had a low-grade headache.

He held it in his hand for a moment before putting it down. “Sherlock analyzed the contents of Jessie’s stomach. The last meal she had was mussels.” He smiled at me. “We did some digging, sorry about that,” he grinned. “Anyway we took another look of the men in Jessie’s life including Father Mark. He was transferred from a Boston church for what they called an ‘inappropriate relationship’ with a parishioner. Turns out he had an affair with some girl, got her pregnant and paid for her to go live in another state until she had the baby and adopted it out.”

“Poor Jessie. But how did you know I was there and in trouble?”

“Well,” he grinned at me, “turns out that a shipment of fresh mussels was delivered to Father Mark a couple of months ago. Only they weren’t so fresh. Turns out they were tainted with saxitoxin. A red flag went up on the CDC website and someone from the environmental protection agency tried to get them back. Father Mark told them he put them down the garbage disposal. Not the right way to dispose of them by the way. Their agency contacted us to follow up. Once we knew that Jessie died after eating mussels we found out from his housekeeper she cooked mussels in butter for Father Mark on the day Jessie died." He sat down in the chair next to the bed. "Millie told us that he wanted mussels cooked for a dinner he was having with you. We put it together, raced here and here you are, safe and sound." I started crying. My emotions were all over the place. "It's okay, Mel, he's in custody. He'll pay for what he did."

"But it was such a stupid way for her to die. He didn't know her like I did. She wasn't going to tell on him. She would pretend the father was some celebrity or a sperm donor and raise the baby as a single parent."

"You can't look at it that way Mel. You have to let it go. You can't change the past you can only go forward from here."

I turned my face to the side away from him. I wasn't sure I wanted to go forward. What did I have left? My job was gone, Cindy still wasn't talking to me only because I accused her ex-husband of abusing Jessie, Jessie was gone and Byron was…what? I closed my eyes wishing I had a time travel machine and could go back a few months and see Jessie again.

"Sleeping, Mel?" Byron wanted to know. I ignored him. He left soon after that.

* * *

Father Mark was arraigned and charged with First Degree Murder and Attempted Murder. He entered the pleas of Not Guilty on both charges which meant he was going to trial. Reporters started calling my hospital room pretending to be long-lost relatives. I finally asked the nurses to take the phone out of my room. In two days I was weak but able to go home.

Much to my surprise, Cindy walked into the hospital room dangling car keys on the end of her finger.

"Ready to go, Mel?" I sat on the end of the bed. My day nurse had just handed me my discharge summary and I was tucking it into my pocket since I didn't have my bag with me.

"You're driving me home?" I asked.

She nodded."Yep. And before you ask, I forgive you. You were just doing your job. Thanks for not dying, Mel." She raced over to me and gave me a big hug.

Tears sprang to my eyes. "No problem," I said. "Did you bring my cane?"

She grinned. "You get a wheeled escort out," she said, snapping her fingers. AJ came in with a wheelchair. I froze not certain what he was going to say.

"I'm still pissed at you for thinking I'd abuse Jessie, but I guess I have to let it go now that Cindy and I are back together," he said, looking at Cindy. "Hope you're feeling better by Saturday, we're counting on you and Byron to stand up for us. Two o'clock sharp."

"At St. Matt's?" I hobbled over to the wheelchair and sat down in it.

"No, at the courthouse," Cindy said. "I never want to see that place again."

"It's not the church's fault, its Father Mark's," I said. "He started having sex with her when she was in middle school. He gave her the hand-carved crucifix because she was his special girl." I shuddered. "Poor Jessie, I wish she would've told us." Cindy gazed out the window instead of at me. "What?" I asked her. She turned her gaze back.

"She told me, she said she didn't want to go to church anymore. She said Father Mark was mean. She cried every time she had to go to classes with him."

"She didn't say he was molesting her though," AJ said. "It's not your fault, Cin." He went over to her and put an arm around her kissing her cheek.

"I'm her mother, I should've known," Cindy said.

"He hid it, that's what pedophiles do," I said.

"At least he's going to jail this time," AJ said.

"What do you mean, 'this time?'" Cindy asked.

"Guess he was kicked out of the Boston parish for getting a young girl pregnant," AJ said.

"How do you know?" Cindy asked.

"It was in the paper this morning." He picked up a newspaper that had been lying on a chair. He held it open for me and Cindy to read the headline.

"Local Priest charged with Murder," I read aloud.

"Keep reading," AJ urged me. He handed me the newspaper. I skimmed the rest of the article. Women in their twenties were coming forward with abuse stories. His former parish in Boston confirmed that a young girl had gotten pregnant by Father Mark. He was given counseling and transferred. To Beechton. I handed the paper to Cindy who gave it back to AJ.

"I don't want to read anymore about him," Cindy said. "How could he do what he did and then look me in the eye?"

"He didn't think he was doing anything wrong," I said. "I've heard pedophiles say that what they do is not wrong, it's love. They do what they do because they love the child and that it's just like any other relationship."

"That is sick," AJ said.

I wanted to change the subject. "Hey, did you guys hear I now own half of Barre? Me along with a three year old boy."

"What are you going to do with a strip club?" AJ wanted to know. "I hope you give discounts." Cindy hit his arm with her fist but she was smiling. At that moment a nurse walked in.

"Still here?" she asked.

"We're just leaving," AJ said, starting to wheel me out. At the elevators Cindy pushed the down button.

"You never said if you'd be at the wedding on Saturday or not," she said.

"I'll try and be there," I said. The elevator dinged, the doors opened and Byron stepped out.

"I thought I missed you," he said. "The nurse said you'd already gone. I went back down to catch you. I decided to come back up and ask exactly when you left and here you are."

"Yup, here I am," I said. He kissed me on the cheek. He said hello to Cindy and AJ.

"AJ and Cindy are getting married on Saturday at the courthouse," I said.

Byron smiled. "Am I invited?"

"Yes, of course," Cindy said. "It's at two."

"I'll be there," he said, smiling at me.

"Don't get any ideas, Williams," I said. Cindy pressed the down button again. I held up my hand. "Hang on a moment. Let's catch the next one. Hand me my bag." I dug in my bag and pulled out a piece of paper I handed it to Cindy.

"What's this?" she asked unfolding it. She laughed. I gave AJ the go-ahead. He pushed the down button again.

"What is it?" AJ asked.

"My half of the strip club," I said. "Think of it as an early wedding present or an early baby gift." Byron whistled.

"Thanks," AJ said. "I didn't think you liked me that much."

"I don't," I said.

"Give AJ a break, Mel. He's learning to channel his anger in a more positive way now," Cindy said as she pressed the button that would take us to the first floor lobby.

"I'm taking up knitting," he said as he wheeled me into the elevator. The four of us laughed.

ACKNOWLEDGMENTS

Thanks to my critique partners, beta readers and readers. Thanks to my agent, Lindsay Leggett at The Rights Factory for her encouragement in getting this uploaded.

ABOUT THE AUTHOR

Kathleen describes herself as an urban Faerie born without wings.
In her messenger bag she carries salt, a vial of dead man's blood, and holy water; a sonic screwdriver, a talking red wax lion, a floral bonnet, a box of Twinkles and a dog-eared copy of *Frankenstein*.

She writes young adult fantasy, gothic horror, historical and historical fantasy and contemporary as well as adult.

Books are available both in eBooks and print form from wherever you like to buy your books!.

CONNECT WITH KATHLEEN HERE:

Twitter: @kathleea
Amazon Author Page:
www.amazon.com/Kathleen-S.-Allen
Pinterest: www.pinterest.com/kathleea
Website:
www.kathleensallen.weebly.com
Blog:
www.kathleensallen.wordpress.com

Made in the USA
Columbia, SC
13 August 2022

65290013R00157